THE BREAKING

NORTHERN WITCH #3

By K.S. Marsden

K.S.M

The Northern Witch Series

Winter Trials (Northern Witch #1)

Awaken (Northern Witch #2)

The Breaking (Northern Witch #3)

Summer Sin (Northern Witch #4)

Printed by Amazon

ISBN: 9798624604605

Chapter One

Sometimes in life, you can look back to one moment in time and say this – this is what caused it. Caused all the pain and the drama.

The first time I saw Damian, I knew that I was in trouble.

The first time I saw Eadric, standing before me on the moors...

Mark stood, the wind buffeting, and pulling at his heavy coat. It whipped tears from his eyes, leaving a cold streak down his face.

Nothing mattered, though, except the potential demon in front of him. He looked so very human, if a little unusual with his long brown hair and coarsely-woven tunic. Only the black eyes gave him away.

"Silvaticus?"

His arm ached, where he'd cut the demon's mark into his own skin. Fresh fear thrummed through Mark's veins, he couldn't deal with this now, alone and helpless. Almost helpless... in response to his terror, Luka appeared at Mark's side, a warm and comforting presence. Mark chanced a glance at the spirit animal – the dog was relaxed, not reading Silvaticus as a threat.

The demon's black eyes faded, replaced by a dazzling green. The young man's expression softened.

"Aye, he's in here. Slivaticus is wēriġ, he slæ now. *Slæ*." Eadric stressed the last word, at Mark's look of confusion.

"Oh, *sleep*. He's weary...?" Mark tried to translate. It was hardly comforting news.

Eadric eyed Mark warily. "Yer th' witch?"

"Aye. I mean: yes, I'm the witch." Mark brushed away the last trace of tears. He hardly believed his eyes. "Are you... really here? Now? This isn't another vision?"

Eadric stepped towards him, reaching about before Mark could think to stagger away. Eadric's hand rested on his shoulder, warm, heavy, and definitely real.

Mark began to shiver at the impossibility of it. "H-how are you here?"

"Ye summoned us." Eadric frowned as he repeated himself.

"I know, but..." Mark trailed off. This broke every rule he knew... did demons have different rules?

Suddenly feeling out of his depth, Mark pulled out his phone and called Nanna. He quickly explained the

6

situation, and was met with silence. "Nanna, are you there?"

"Yes." Nanna snapped, before falling silent again. "See if you can get him to follow you to the yard. I'll meet you there."

The line went dead, and Mark was left staring at his phone.

He wasn't the only one – Eadric looked at the device curiously. Mark realised that it was something beyond his understanding. "It's a phone, so I can talk to my Nanna. She's another witch – she'd like to meet you."

"Witchcræft?" Eadric asked, his eyes still fixed on the phone.

"Yeah, sure." Mark agreed, shoving the mobile into his pocket. "Will you come with me to the stables?"

"Aye, lead the way."

Mark started to walk slowly across the moors, taking the direct route to the yard. He eyed Eadric as subtly as possible, half-expecting the demon to rear his ugly head and attack him.

Eadric was a couple of inches shorter than Mark, but he was just as broad across the shoulder. He was wearing the same tunic and trousers from the vision, looking like he had literally stepped out of the 14th Century.

Mark marched on. With his fear waning, it wasn't long before Luka vanished, no longer needing to protect him. Mark's gaze stayed locked on the other man.

"Do you... remember me?" He finally asked.

7

"Aye." Eadric's gentle green eyes turned on him, considering his answer. "At first I thought you wer' a dream. An engel sent to help me, but Silvaticus kan that engels arn'y real. Then ye came agin, I knew ye wer' real..."

Unable to shake the feeling that he was currently in a dream, Mark reached out, his hand touching the very firm, and very real arm of his new acquaintance. Eadric shot him a strange look.

"Sorry, I had to check you were definitely here. This is crazy." Mark couldn't take his eyes off the man. Sure, he was as ruggedly handsome in person, as he was in the visions; but Mark was more distracted by the demon that Eadric shared his soul with. "How did you end up harbouring a demon?"

Eadric gave him a grim smile, "Why did ye summon him?"

"Robert." Mark replied, thinking how the demon possessing Damian had left him with no choice.

"Robert." Eadric echoed, his voice laced with pain.

Eadric didn't offer any more information, and Mark didn't want to pry further. They fell into an uncomfortable silence, as they marched along the gentle slopes of the moors.

The steel roof of the barn came into view, and Mark followed the familiar trail. At this time of day, all the horses were out in the field and the stables were completely still.

Mark gave a sigh of relief when he saw Nanna's Land Rover sitting in the yard. The doors opened, and out stepped Nanna. She was quickly followed by fellow-witches, Denise and Danny. Nanna had clearly decided that this needed reinforcements.

The old woman marched across the yard, her eyes fixed on the potential threat.

"Eadric, this is Nanna." Mark introduced, light-headed at how surreal this was.

Nanna brushed passed him, leaning uncomfortably close to Eadric. She inspected his green eyes for several long moments, her magic coursing between them. Eventually, Nanna leant back, apparently satisfied with what she had seen.

"Eadric said that Silvaticus was exhausted, that he's dormant." Mark said, trying to help.

"Hmph, we'll see about that." Nanna remarked. "Get your new friend in the car."

When Mark opened the door for him, Eadric looked suspiciously at the vehicle. "Is this ye carriage? D'ye need aide w'the hosses?"

Mark gestured for him to get in. Once everyone had piled into the old car, Nanna started the engine.

Eadric jumped at the noise, looking to Mark for an explanation.

"It's a... magic carriage." Mark offered, ignoring the derisive snort from Danny.

Eadric's expression changed to sheer terror when the car lurched forwards and bounced down the road in response to Nanna's aggressive driving.

Mark still couldn't take his eyes off Eadric. He didn't sense any danger, despite the sleeping demon. Squished into the back seat of Nanna's car with Danny, they travelled in tense silence.

After a short journey, Mark looked up to see an unfamiliar house looming in front of them.

"Where-?"

"Mi casa es tu casa." Denise trilled from the front seat.

Mark guessed it must have been closer than their house. He got out, noticing that Eadric was shadowing his movements in this alien, futuristic world.

The inside of Denise's house was as bright and colourful as Mark imagined. It was eclectic and messy, and perfectly-Denise.

Nanna tried to quiz Eadric, but the language barrier left them both confused.

Nanna sighed and turned to Danny, "He's all yours. See what you can get out of him."

Mark felt a stab of envy as Danny proved himself a useful ally for Nanna, again. The history professor took Eadric over to some mis-matched chairs, and they were soon deep in conversation.

Denise brought out some herbal tea, which Mark dutifully sipped.

"I thought we'd take Eadric home – I mean, our home." Mark glanced over at their guest.

"Not until we know what we're dealing with." Nanna cautioned. "Damian and his demon have spent too much time with us, I don't want to risk their demonic essence causing a reaction in this… new demon."

"You do seem to attract them, deary." Denise cooed.

Danny eventually wandered back, with Eadric on his heels.

"His name is Eadric Stoneman. The demon he carries is called Silvaticus, and seems to have a history with the Stoneman family after possessing his grand-father and great-grandfather before him. It seems to be a… mutually beneficial relationship; Silvaticus gets to exist on our plane, and the Stoneman host gets the strengths of a demon."

Nanna sighed, "It's not the first time I've heard of people being wooed by the dark powers. What excuse does this boy have?"

"A common enemy: Duke *Robert*."

"Robert? As in, our Robert?"

Danny gave a sorry smile. "It appears so."

"I guess that explains why he's here." Nanna muttered. "But not *how*."

Danny shrugged. "Eadric couldn't describe it, other than magic. We'll have to wait for Silvaticus to be strong enough to answer those questions."

Nanna and Denise shared a meaningful look.

11

"If you don't want him here..." Nanna started, before her friend cut her off.

"It's the best place for him, if Danny's the only one who can communicate easily with him." Denise poked Nanna's arm. "Besides, deary, you are not the only powerful witch in this county. Me and boyo can handle Silvaticus, if he pops his head up."

Mark squirmed in his seat. He had personally seen how powerful Denise and her son were, but that didn't forgive the fact that he was the reason there was a demon in their house.

Nanna seemed to be experiencing a similar guilt. "All the same, I'll ask some of the coven to stop by and check on our... guest."

Mark didn't say a word on the drive home. He was still processing the fact that the guy from his visions had crossed centuries and was *here*. With another *demon*.

The rumble of the old car was the perfect background for the questions that pummelled him.

The further they got from Eadric, the more reality returned. Mark remembered with painful clarity, why he'd been on the moors in the first place.

Damian had left him.

The pain struck anew.

Mark had always thought that people were being dramatic when they moaned about being broken-hearted. The reality was harsh, the raw pain threatening to overwhelm him.

Nanna was on his heels, herding him into his house. Mark's parents looked up warily, ready to deal with the next dose of trouble.

It was startling, that this was the new normal for his family, when Mark had never (or almost-never) misbehaved. He'd never been in trouble at school, or grounded, and he couldn't even remember any significant argument.

That his usually-chilled Dad was already looking disappointed, only added to Mark's dark mood.

"What happened?" His Mum asked.

"Nanna can explain." He said gruffly, his courage failing. "I'm going to my room."

Before his parents could protest, Mark stomped upstairs, slamming the door behind him.

His phone blared out, making him jump. He glanced at the screen, his heart leaping at the sight of 'Damian – Home'. Mark hit the answer button so hard, he nearly broke his thumb.

"Damian?" Mark gasped.

"Hi, Mark? It's Maggie, Damian's aunt…"

"Oh, hi Miss Cole." Mark replied, not even trying to keep the disappointment out of his voice.

"Have you seen Damian? Is he with you?" She asked in a rush of words.

"No, he called this morning to… say goodbye."

Aunt Maggie swore so creatively, it made Mark blush.

"Sorry, I'm still getting used to playing the responsible adult." Maggie followed up. "Damian left me a letter, a bloody letter, that's all I'm worth after… sorry, I don't mean to rant."

"That's OK." Mark mumbled. "What did Damian have to say?"

"Not much, he was being vague and said he had to leave." Maggie sighed audibly, the sound causing the phone line to crackle. "I thought… I thought he was settling in and enjoying life. I'd never seen him so happy, he had football and friends, and he had you… Then I had to go and ruin it."

"What?"

"It's the only reason that makes sense. I'd created a home where Damian could finally feel safe after everything he's been through, then I went and ruined it by letting Miriam stay overnight. It was inappropriate and too fast, but I didn't mean to. I guess I got swept up in the moment and I confess I forgot about Damian…"

"Woah, it's not your fault." Mark interrupted, when it became clear Maggie had plenty more self-flagellation to share.

"It's not?" Maggie asked, her voice shaking.

"Damian was cool with you and Miriam."

"He was?"

"Yeah. I mean, he wasn't about to suggest double-dating; but he was happy that you'd found someone nice after your douchebag boyfriend." Mark replied, knowing that he might be stretching the truth a little. The revelation about Maggie and her first girlfriend had inconveniently come right before Robert took over and all hell broke loose.

"Then why did he leave?" Maggie insisted. "I knew he kept secrets... I didn't think they'd drive him away."

Mark groaned; how many times had he told Damian to tell his aunt about Robert. Mark didn't think he had the right to confess about the demon Damian had been harbouring for months.

"I can't share his secrets, Maggie. Just know that, he thinks he's protecting you."

"He's *sixteen*, it's my job to protect him, not the other way around." Maggie fumed. "I've got half a mind to go down to London and drag him back by his blond highlights."

"London? You think that's where he's gone?" Mark asked.

Maggie sighed, "Yes, I found a search for train tickets on the computer. I wished I'd noticed in time to stop him..."

"I'm sorry..." Mark made a poor attempt at being sympathetic.

"Well, if you hear anything, please let me know." Maggie begged, before making an awkward goodbye.

Mark trembled as the call ended. Damian had to realise how many people cared for him, and now Mark knew where to find him. The capital was a big and daunting thing, somewhere that Mark had only ever seen on screen. The idea of going alone was terrifying.

Mark's phone rang again, and he was tempted to throw it across the room. He was exhausted and wanted to be left alone.

When Sarah's name flashed up on the screen, Mark froze. This was the first time she'd contacted him, since he'd called her a liar, when she'd claimed to witness Damian kissing Michelle. Mark burnt with guilt that he'd made the mistake of trusting his new demon-possessed boyfriend over his lifelong friends.

"Sarah, hi."

"Hello, Mark." Sarah replied tersely.

There was a long pause, and Mark feared that she would hang up.

"Thanks for calling, I… need you guys."

"You always do. Wasn't that the problem?" Sarah sighed. "You've really hurt Harry."

"How's he doing?" Mark asked, not sure if he wanted the answer.

"He's feeling pretty betrayed. I've just come from his place, and he's miserable. You've got a long way to go to make it up to him."

"Oh, too soon to ask for help…"

"What help?" Sarah asked, exasperated.

"Damian's done another runner." Mark admitted, quietly. "He thinks he's protecting us, but the safest place for him is *here*."

Sarah groaned. "Again? Seriously? When a guy keeps running away from you, you need to take the hint."

"So, you guys won't help?"

"Not a chance." Sarah replied firmly.

"Even if it means an impromptu roadtrip to London?"

"London?" Sarah echoed.

"Yeah, his aunt thinks he's bolted for his old home." Mark reasoned.

"Well… I suppose a trip to London wouldn't be too bad…" Sarah paused. "*If* you can fix things with Harry."

Mark swore, it would be so much easier if he could just kidnap him. Maybe there was a magical spell that could help heal their friendship.

"When I left, his mum was forcing homemade stew on him. Now is the time to strike."

Mark flinched at the memory of Mrs Johnson's cooking, now that certainly was a special potion. Sarah was right, Harry would be upset by the food, and Mark could start to earn his trust again.

Chapter Two

Mark stood outside Harry's bedroom window, his bike discarded in the dark garden.

He didn't have a boombox, but he did have a pizza in one hand and his phone in the other. He pressed play, and Harry's favourite track blasted out.

The Arctic Monkeys had been the first live gig Mark and Harry experienced, when they were wide-eyed fourteen-year-old lads. Two years later, the band's music still resonated with them, and it always would. It was a time before girlfriends and boyfriends, magic and demons; when they were two best friends trying to negotiate the rocky path of being teenage boys.

"Harry!" Mark yelled above the noise.

The neighbour's dog started barking, just out of time with the music. Harry's curtains opened and yellow light poured into the garden.

Harry appeared in the window, then froze. "What the hell…"

"Look, Harry, I know that I'm not John Cusack; but I know this is your favourite movie. Even though you only pretend to watch it because of Sarah. I was hoping… you'd give me another chance."

"Shut off that racket!" A shout from next door split the air.

Harry flushed red with embarrassment.

"Well?" Mark asked, his arms growing tired as he continued to hold the pizza box and phone aloft.

Harry looked torn, and Mark began to hope.

"What pizza is it?"

"Meat feast with stuffed crust." Mark bellowed over the music, the barking dog and the shouting neighbour. He held his breath.

"Fine, you best come in."

"Yes!" Mark turned the track off, and headed to the door before Harry could change his mind.

Harry's house was as familiar as his own; Mark let himself into the kitchen, passing a surprised-looking set of parents in the living room.

"Hi Mr Johnson, Mrs Johnson."

"Hi, Mark dear. Glad to see you're back in his lordship's good graces. Harry is upstairs." Harry's mum replied.

"Thanks, Mrs Johnson."

Mark ran up the stairs as fast as he could, whilst juggling a pizza.

Just as Mark went to knock, Harry's door opened. His best friend snatched the pizza box out of Mark's hand, turning back to his room.

Mark followed him in. The bedroom was unusually tidy, which was always a sign Sarah had been there, as Harry never made the effort to tidy his room for Mark.

When Harry silently sat on the floor and opened the box, Mark took it as an invitation to join him.

It took three slices of pizza before the tension in Harry's shoulders ebbed and he deigned to look at Mark.

"Y'know this doesn't make up for what you've done." Harry said gruffly.

"But it's a start. I'll do whatever it takes. I'll come to all of your gigs; I'll be your roadie and be at your beck and call."

Harry gave a little, half-amused snort. "So, what's new with you?"

"Damian broke up with me, and... there might be another demon on the scene." Mark admitted.

"He broke – wait, what?" Harry choked on a lump of stuffed crust. "*Another* demon?"

"Yeah, the one who helped us escape the other night. He's still seeking vengeance against Damian's demon." Mark took a deep breath. "I'm really sorry, I should have listened to you. I never should've invoked an unknown demon, it's pure luck he's on our side."

"Oh, for all that's holy – *shut up!*" Harry snapped, running his hands through his hair in desperation. "Demons are bad, Mark. I can't believe you even need

20

teaching that! There's no such thing as 'good' demons or 'demons that are on our side'."

"Oh, and I suppose you're the expert." Mark retorted, before he could remind himself not to argue.

"I might not be a witch, *mate*; but I witnessed everything those demons did." Harry reasoned. "Forgive me, but at what point in all those attacks, did the demons come across as 'good guys'?"

Mark swallowed his response, unable to argue against Harry's logic.

It was hope alone that made him trust Silvaticus. Well, that and his choice of vessel. Eadric had such an aura of goodness around him… unless Mark was just being fooled by a handsome face.

"Fine. You're right, I'm wrong." Mark muttered. "I need my head checking."

Harry grunted in agreement, then left to get drinks. When he returned, he threw a can of coke at Mark, harder than necessary.

"So, why'd Damian dump you? Was he finally fed up with you being a goodie-two-shoes?"

Mark winced. "He's trying to protect me from Robert, but the last time he ran away to protect someone, he nearly died."

The memories were still vivid, of finding Damian half-frozen in the middle of a snowstorm. Hadn't his boyfriend – ex-boyfriend – learnt that running away was dangerous.

"I need to find him." Mark said, his voice cracking. "I know I don't deserve your help right now, but you're the only one I want to turn to."

Harry looked slightly mollified at the compliment of being needed. He played distractedly with his coke can, drawing the moment out dramatically.

"Fine, but you owe me big." He conceded. "Where do we go to find your fella?"

"London."

"London?" Harry brightened at the prospect, having never gone anywhere bigger than Leeds. "What are we waiting for, let's go."

Mark smiled at his friend's eager response. "We can jump on a train tomorrow morning. Meet you at Tealford station first thing?"

"Deal. I'll have to let Sarah know; she's always wanted to go to London – she'll never forgive us if we leave her behind."

Mark nodded, biting his tongue. Harry didn't need to know that Mark had already discussed this with his girlfriend, before him.

Chapter Three

Monday morning was the first real day of half-term, when Mark would normally revel in not being in school. Today, he was a bundle of nerves. He watched his parents rushing through their weekday-morning routine, whilst Mark tried to appear as nonchalant as possible. He thought it was working until his Mum asked if he had stomach-ache.

"Um, sort of." He confessed. "I'm going to meet Harry and Sarah today, try and mend some bridges."

"Oh, that's fantastic, darling." His Mum cooed, pulling him into an awkward, one-armed hug, as she tried to balance her coffee. "Just grovel and apologise for everything, and it will be alright."

"Hey, you're supposed to be on my side." Mark frowned at her reaction.

His Mum kissed his forehead. "Mark, I love you; but Harry is like a surrogate son to me. I can't have favourites, especially after *you* screwed up."

"Love you, too." Mark reluctantly grumbled.

Mark waited for his parents to leave the house, the sound of their cars quickly disappearing for another unexciting day; before he grabbed his coat and pulled his bike out of the garage.

It was another cold and miserable February morning, but at least the rain was holding off, as Mark cycled down the country lanes, trying to ignore the cars that whizzed by too close. It was only a few miles to Tealford train station, but Mark had a quick stop to make, first.

With a little help from the maps-app on his phone, Mark was soon cycling up to Denise's house, the traditional stone building masking the kooky interior from the world.

Not quite sure what he was going to say, he knocked and waited.

Before long, the door opened to reveal Denise. Her previously-green hair was now a bright turquoise colour, and twisted into curling rags that looked like they had been pulled from a patchwork quilt. She blinked up at Mark for a few moments. "Mark, what a lovely surprise. No Nanna with ye?"

"Um, no, just me." Mark shrugged. "I'm going out of town today, and I wanted to check how Eadric – I mean, the new demon, is doing..."

24

Denise waved him in, towards the kitchen, where a pot of her herbal tea sat brewing. Without asking, she poured Mark a generous cupful. "He's doing alright. That young man has had a lot to take in, but he seems like a nice chap. No sign of his demon, yet; but Eadric seems oddly fond of him."

Mark nursed his cup of herbal tea, not in a rush to actually drink it again. "Where is he?"

"Oh, he's just getting ready. I confess Eadric's rather enchanted by our 'magic' shower, he was in there for an hour yesterday. He'll be down for breakfast in a bit." Denise said with a chuckle.

Mark couldn't help but smile at the thought of Eadric coping with the modern world he'd been thrust into. His smile froze into an awkward twisted thing, as Eadric walked in.

Eadric's brown hair was wet and plastered to his forehead. He was buckling a belt onto some borrowed jeans, that hung low enough to show the top of his black boxers. And he wore little else. His torso was sculpted muscle from a life of labour, and Mark found it impossible to look away.

Denise coughed, less-than-subtly, then chuckled at Mark's reaction. "You remind me so much of your Nanna: easily distracted by a handsome guy."

Mark was about to argue, but the memory of Nanna openly crooning about her crush on the farrier made him blush.

"Mark!" Eadric exclaimed, breaking into a grin. "Gōdne mergen. Do ye break fast wi' us?"

"Um, no, I've already eaten." Mark said, before Denise could ply him with potentially-kooky food. "I wanted to check you were alright, before I... well, I'm hoping to track down my boyfriend today, I'm not sure how long it will take."

"Have you heard from him?" Denise asked, sounding hopeful. "Miriam says that poor Maggie is falling apart since he left; that boy needs to come home to his aunt."

"No," Mark admitted, painfully. "But I have a few ideas where he might be."

"Boy...friend?" Eadric echoed, confused by the term.

"The boy that Mark is courtin'." Denise said with a dismissive wave of her hand.

Eadric's confusion didn't lighten.

"Courting means-"

"I ken." Eadric interrupted, looking embarrassed. "Tis agin domas."

Mark blinked, not understanding him. He looked to Denise for an explanation, but she just shrugged.

"Sometimes I can figure them out, but that's a 'Danny phrase'." She pulled out a small notepad and jotted it down. "I'll ask him when he comes round later."

Mark looked at his watch, as much as he wanted to stay and learn more about the strange new man that had come crashing into their lives; his best friends were waiting at the train station for him, ready to hunt down Damian.

"I've really got to go. Can you message me, if you learn anything important?" Mark asked.

"Sure thing, deary. You go bring your boyfriend back."

Chapter Four

Mark thought there was nothing more exciting than simply having Harry back on his side. His mind was changed, as the train whisked the three of them closer and closer to London. Going on an adventure with two of his best friends, was even better.

The carriage getting more and more packed at each stop, commuters and tourists pouring on for their ride to London on a Monday morning.

Harry had put dibs on the window seat, and all three of them leant over, excited to spot the familiar landmarks for the first time in real life.

Eventually, they pulled into Kings Cross, and moved with a flood of people marching to their destination.

"OK, we're here. What now?" Harry asked.

"The London Dungeon? A walk along the South Bank?" Sarah piped up, her voice higher than normal. "Ooh, *please* can we go on the London Eye?"

"I meant – where do we find Damian?" Harry corrected.

"Oops, sorry." Sarah blushed as she recalled their main mission.

"Damian used to live in Bexley. His house was sold since... y'know, his parents died; but his grandmother's house is still there. I stake anything *that's* where he's hiding out." Mark reeled off, wishing he felt as confident as he sounded.

He didn't know for sure that Damian would go to his late grandmother's house. He'd only lived there for two weeks, before she too had succumbed to the demon's curse, dying from a heart attack. Yet, the vacant house was left to Damian, her only surviving relative. It was the perfect bolthole.

"We'll have to go on the underground, then take the train to Bexley." Mark said nervously, as they hovered at the top of the longest escalator he'd ever seen.

He took a deep breath to try and get rid of the sudden rush of vertigo.

"Let's go." Harry announced, pushing past without a care.

The three of them stuck close together, until another commuter stood behind Mark and huffed loudly. Not sure what he'd done wrong, Mark gaped at the angry-looking woman.

Rather than speak, she jerked her head in the direction of a row of signs saying: 'stand on the right, walk on the left'.

Hardly believing that such a minor thing could matter, Mark edged to the other side of the steps.

The strange woman huffed angrily again, then stormed past, followed by a never-ending stream of people.

Mark blushed at his faux pas, and fixed his gaze on the adverts that played on small screens, until it made him feel dizzy. Finally at the bottom, Mark staggered away.

"This way?" He said uncertainly.

Mark and his friends finally found the platforms and joined the crush of people waiting.

"Excuse me, is this th' train t'London Bridge?" Mark asked a young businessman scrolling through his phone.

The young man stared at him, and Mark wondered if he'd sprouted horns.

"London Bridge?" Mark repeated.

The man looked increasingly harried and his eyes flicked up to a black screen with orange writing. "Yes…" He said pointedly, then turned back to his phone.

"Thanks." Mark muttered. Londoners were very peculiar creatures.

The rest of the journey went relatively smoothly, and less than an hour later they arrived at their destination. Bexley seemed like a nice area, both quaint and busy. As though someone had taken the quintessential English village and dropped it in the middle of a heaving London estate.

"There's green stuff!" Harry remarked, staring at the wooded areas with wide eyes.

"Yeah, they're called trees. We have them in Yorkshire." Mark teased.

"No, I just... thought everythin' inside the M25 were grey; all concrete an' tarmac..."

Sarah gave a brief laugh at her boyfriend's odd remark. "Where on earth did you get that idea?"

Mark smiled at the exchange; he had missed this. He'd been so caught up in Damian, and his witch-training, it felt like an age since they last joked around.

Every step they took towards the grandmother's house, was a reminder of their mission and the light mood quickly evaporated. As they walked down the street, Mark spotted a 'For Sale' sign standing lopsided in the small, paved front yard. There was no sign of life in the detached house, the dark windows a blur of grey curtains.

Mark hung back, his hope quickly fading.

Sarah pushed past, rattling the front door handle. "Locked. Can you alohomora it?"

"Aloh- this isn't bloody Harry Potter." Mark muttered. He was a *real* witch, who performed *real* magic... Mark's train of thought faltered, he was a witch-in-training – there might be a spell to unlock the door, that he hadn't learnt yet.

"Let's try round the back." Harry suggested, climbing the wooden fence and disappearing.

Mark gave the shorter Sarah a boost, and followed his friends into the back yard. The garden had an uncared-for look, the dull plants still in their winter hibernation.

"We're in luck; we're not the first to break in." Harry piped up, looking through a smashed pane in the back door. He gingerly put his arm through, and felt around until he hit the lock. Harry grinned, "We're in!"

The house was cold and full of shadows, the air stale and damp after months of being empty. The old-fashioned furniture was covered in dust.

"It doesn't look like Damian's here." Sarah whispered, her voice breaking through the silence.

Mark sighed, stirring dust into the air. "I need to check upstairs."

He walked through the shadowy dining room, and found the stairs. There were three bedrooms, as soon as Mark stepped into one, he knew that it belonged to Damian. The walls were red, the paint fresh, compared to the fusty flowery wallpaper in the other rooms. There were boxes of stuff, Mark guessed they were non-essential things that either Damian didn't want, or he couldn't fit into Aunt Maggie's tiny cottage.

The thin layer of dust had been disturbed, the boxes moved around.

"Someone's been here…" Mark noted, thumbing through a box of clothes.

"Even if it was Damian, he's not here now." Sarah said from the doorway. She sighed loudly. "What's the back-up plan?"

32

"I'm kinda glad it didn't work out." Harry confessed. "I mean, I want to find Damian; but what if we stumble into Robert? Are we prepared to face a demon?"

Mark paused, he'd been so keen to plough ahead, he hadn't really considered this. He shrugged, then realised that wasn't the most solid argument. "I've faced him before, and came out on top. Besides, I can't imagine he's recovered from the battle."

Harry looked at him sceptically, "Oh wow, now I feel safe."

Harry grunted, as his girlfriend punched his arm.

Mark shook his head, the entire history of their friendship involved Harry causing trouble, and Mark going along to mediate. "I can't believe you're playing the voice of reason."

"Well, you seem to be taking over the role of careless troublemaker…" Harry replied, an unusual edge to his voice.

"Come on, let's get out of here, before we get done for breaking and entering." Sarah interrupted, impatiently tugging at Harry's sleeve.

"Technically, we didn't break in." Harry argued.

"I really don't think that will hold up in court." Sarah rolled her eyes, "So, what now?"

Mark reluctantly followed his friends down the stairs of the abandoned house. He thumbed a piece of material in his pocket. He had a magical back-up plan, but there was one more mundane route he wanted to try.

"Damian's best friend… their family lives just round the corner."

"I thought 'is best mate was in a coma…?" Harry asked.

"Yes, she is; but her parents might know something."

Mark's comment was met with a deafening silence; he'd not managed to impress the others with his plan.

Back outside, the cool wind was refreshing after dust-filled air of the abandoned house.

Mark led the others onto the street. After failing to find Damian, they had lost their light-hearted banter; the only voice was from Mark's mobile app, directing them to the right house.

This time, there was a car in the driveway, and the sound of a TV drifted through an open window.

A tall man answered the door, his black hair greying and tired circles beneath his eyes. He looked down at Mark and his friends with mild disinterest. "Whatever you're collecting for, we're not interested."

"M-mr Lykaois?" Mark rushed, before the older guy closed the door on them. "We're friends of Damian."

The man paused, looking at them, as though for the first time. "Why didn't you say so? Come in, come in!"

Sharing a look with Harry at Mr Lykaois' sudden joviality, Mark smiled and stepped into the house.

"Anthea, Damian's friends are here!" Mr Lykaois called out, his voice betraying his Mediterranean heritage, now that he was relaxed. "Come into the kitchen and have a drink, you can catch us up on everything Damian is doing."

"You haven't seen him recently?" Mark asked, his heart dropping further.

"Not since he moved away to live with his aunt. I had hoped he would come visit during the Christmas holidays, but... I guess he's got no real reason to come back to London, since..." Mr Lykaois' good humour faltered, but he hid it with a strained smile and gestured to introduce his wife.

Anthea Lykaois was a similarly bright-eyed woman; who appeared soft and warm. "The kettle is on, make yourself comfortable."

Mark was reminded of the welcoming feel, every time he stepped into Nanna's kitchen. Mrs Lykaois' kitchen filled the house with warm, delicious smells, that made Mark's stomach rumble.

"Oh my, when was the last time you ate?" Anthea asked sharply.

"Umm..."

"Sit down, I'll make you all a late lunch." Anthea tutted, "You are all wasting away, far too skinny."

"Thanks." Harry trilled, the first to sit down at the kitchen table, more than happy to be fed by these strangers.

Mr Lykaois set down three mugs of tea in front of them. "You guys don't sound like locals."

"Ah, no, were from Yorkshire." Sarah piped up, "We go t' Tealford school wi' Damian. And Mark is Damian's… I mean…"

She trailed off, clearly not sure if she should be the one to reveal Mark and Damian's relationship. Even Mark wasn't sure how he felt about sharing it with strangers.

"Oooh, Damian got himself a boyfriend?" Mrs Lykaois said, ecstatic at the prospect. She looked over in Mark's direction. "Such a handsome chap, I can't tell you how happy I am!"

"We've known Damian for years." Mr Lykaois explained with a smile. "Even before he was gay."

Before he was gay? Mark couldn't help but glance at his friends at the popular misconception.

The older man didn't miss the silent exchange, but shrugged in response. "You know what I mean – before he came out as gay. Our little Konnie had quite the crush on him, when they were kids. I'm so happy they stayed close; Damian… struggled with friends at school."

Mark stared into his mug of tea, steam rising from the surface. He knew a little about Damian's life in London, how the pupils at his old school gave him grief for his sexual orientation, and only football had provided a safe place. "He's settled in really well at Tealford, he's joined the football team and quickly became the star."

Mrs Lykaois slid some plates on the table, bread, olives and chopped lamb and tomatoes. A colourful array that looked both healthy and traditional.

"Eat, eat!" She insisted.

36

Harry and Sarah readily dug in. Mark put a few pieces on a plate, noticing the waft of herbs.

"What brings you to London?" Mr Lykaois asked.

"Erm, we're looking for Damian. It's a long story, but we think he bolted for home." Mark replied, his guilt suddenly eliminating his appetite. He pushed the bread around his plate, listlessly.

"Do you know where Damian might have gone?" Sarah asked, as she reached for some humous.

"I'm sorry, honey. Damian and Konnie were home birds, they spent their time here, or at his parents' house."

Mark's slither of hope completely vanished. This was a dead end; the only highlight the good food, that Mark couldn't bring himself to eat. He grasped his mug of tea tightly, the aroma was unusual, a different blend to what he was used to, and he could only pretend to sip at it.

Mr and Mrs Lykaois were perfect hosts for their unexpected guests. They treated Mark and his friends as extended family, and chatted openly. They shared stories of Damian's youth, alongside their daughter. Every time they mentioned Konnie, a hint of sadness flashed across their faces.

When it came time to leave, Mrs Lykaois made them promise that they would come back, if they needed somewhere to stay tonight.

Mark was struck by their kindness, and gave her a hug, making Anthea giggle and bat away his sign of affection.

37

"If you see Damian, please let him know that he's always welcome here. He can always visit Konnie, too. She might not know he's there; but I think she'd appreciate it."

Mark walked to the end of the street, out of sight of the Lykaois house.

"So, what now?" Sarah asked.

Harry shrugged, "There's time for sight-seeing before the last train home."

Mark reached into his coat pocket and thumbed a hidden piece of fabric. "I have one last trick." He admitted, pulling it out.

"A ratty old t-shirt?" Harry asked, frowning at the revelation.

"It belonged to Damian. I can do a rough tracking spell with it." Mark explained, trying to sound confident.

"Why didn't you do this before?" Sarah demanded, punching his arm.

"Ow, I thought the punches were reserved for Harry!" Mark moaned, rubbing his bicep. "She hits hard for a little person."

"I've been saying that for *ages*, you never believed me." Harry shrugged.

Mark held up the t-shirt. "I needed something from his time in London. His current wardrobe is an expression of his new life in Yorkshire, there could be a clash of signals."

"Alright, what else do you need?" Sarah asked, jumping on board.

"Somewhere quiet for a few minutes." Mark replied. "I think I saw a little park on the way here."

They found a grassy area, with a cute, man-made pond, and a few trees scattered about. On this grey February afternoon, the place was nearly deserted, save for a few dog-walkers in the distance.

Feeling more than a little awkward at doing this in a public place, Mark sat down, the moisture from the grass soaking through his jeans.

"Is there anything we need to do?" Sarah piped up, a bright look in her eyes, as she watched him get ready to perform magic.

"Not really, no." Mark replied, before rethinking his answer. "Magic can sometimes be boosted by the use of circles. I was just going to use the elements, but you guys can-"

Mark hadn't even chance to finish, before Sarah dropped down on the damp grass next to him. Harry followed a little more reluctantly, grumbling about getting a wet arse.

Mark took their hands, silently grateful for their support. He closed his eyes and tried to clear his mind, finding a quiet and peaceful place to start his spell. The smell of earth intensified as Mark drew on the elements, and he started to feel a familiar sense of calm. He allowed it to wash out, hitting gently against the barrier his friends created, the power bouncing back within their circle.

39

Mark heard Sarah gasp at the sensation. He smiled, remembering the awe he'd felt when he first used magic. Mark pushed the thought aside, and concentrated on the task at hand.

The chant for the spell was simple enough, and Mark was ready; but instead of the rhyming verse, a few solitary words slipped out. "Damian, come back to me."

His voice was barely above a whisper, as his heartache bled into the words.

A tremor of power teased the air, and drops of dew lifted from the grass, hovering above the ground. The clear water became dark, the soil staining into shadowy shapes. The random patterns moved into a sharper definition, and Mark could make out a familiar face. Damian. Even in the sepia tones, he was handsome, though it was impossible to tell if he had blue eyes, or the black eyes of Robert. The image shifted, drawing back, so they could see his immediate location. Mark could make out a sign above a door "Peril" stamped in solid letters; before the magic pulled away, speeding high above the scene. Mark glimpsed that he was North of the Thames, before the map faded.

Having done its work, the spell started to fade; but a new and very different power surged through. Dark magic twisted up within their circle, suddenly exploding. Mark fell backwards and screamed as the t-shirt he clutched burst into flames. He threw it into the circle, and the fire turned gold, then black.

As quickly as it started, it was over. Mark panted for breath, staring into the circle, at a loss to what had happened. The t-shirt was gone, burnt to cinders. Inside the circle, the grass was charred, a symbol glowed, but faded with the embers.

"Please tell me that was supposed to happen?" Harry said, his usual humour rattled by what had occurred.

Mark shook his head, trying to work out what had happened. He recognised the dark, demonic source of the magic; the way it clung to everything, even after the spell dissipated. Had it been a warning, to stay away? Or a challenge? He wished he'd brought Nanna along for answers.

He eyed the fading symbol, committing it to memory. When they got back home, he'd have to see if it was in the *Dictionnaire Infernal* that Denise had leant him.

"I can see why you're so keen on magic; that was a rush!" Sarah announced, getting to her feet and brushing herself off. "Except from that last bit, of course."

"It got out of hand." Mark replied, truthfully enough. He didn't want to admit that was a taste of dark magic at the end; he could already imagine Harry storming off, telling him he'd told him so.

Harry didn't notice Mark's guilty expression; he was on his phone, deep in concentration. "Peril: a trendy bar with live music. It's in Covent Garden."

"Let's go."

Chapter Five

Mark felt like he was finally getting the hang of London transport, as they travelled back across the capital. Familiar sites flicked by, but Mark was less entranced by the sightseeing, when he knew he was on Damian's trail.

Whereas Damian was the southern anomaly at their school in Tealford, here they were surrounded by London accents, with so many other nationalities mixed in.

The three of them walked along the crowded streets. It was already dark, but the post-work Londoners and tourists were still out strong. Even at the end of a dank day in February, London had an undeniable, vibrant energy. Sarah skipped ahead, and the boys couldn't help laughing at her endless enthusiasm.

Walking through Covent Garden, they were surrounded by bars and restaurants. Sitting innocently amongst them, was their target.

Peril was plastered in bold black letters on an ivory background. At first glance, the building was elegant and old-fashioned, probably to appeal to the tourists who didn't know what an English pub looked like. A retro blackboard was propped up outside, with too-perfect writing, announcing today's drink deal, and confirmed that the music drifting out was live.

Mark hesitated, Damian might be inside... did his boyfriend – his ex-boyfriend – really want to be found?

Harry had no such qualms and pushed past, heading for the door. A bored-looking bouncer stepped into his path.

"ID?" He grunted.

"Sure." Harry took a card out of his wallet and flashed it with a calm confidence.

The bouncer frowned down at him. "That's... a school library card..."

"Yeah, but it's a really good photo." Harry reasoned.

The bouncer looked at him, completely bemused. Eventually the big man laughed. "Bugger off, you cheeky sod."

Harry sighed and backed away.

"Look, we don't want to drink, I'm just looking for my friend. Perhaps you've seen him?" Mark argued, pulling out his phone to find a photo of Damian.

"I'm not letting you in, either way." The bouncer said, crossing his arms, not even looking at the picture. "You kids need to scoot. I'm sure there's a Mickey Mouse club somewhere."

Before Mark could respond, he felt Sarah's small hand pulling him away.

"What a jerk." She remarked with a huff. "I don't think we'll get past him without help. Unfortunately, I left my low-cut top at home. Have you got any magic tricks?"

Mark ran through his inventory of spells, which unfortunately didn't take very long. "Nothing, Nanna didn't think to include dodging-bouncer-spells in my training. I guess I could try and invent one..." Mark's voice trailed off, he wasn't very confident that he could make up a spell on the fly. Where would he even start?

The odds changed, as a second bouncer came out of Peril, taking over for the first. Mark eyed the new woman, she looked just as hard-arsed as the man, but at least they effectively had a fresh start. Maybe Mark could come up with a new argument... maybe he could use a spell to cause a mild distraction...

Harry marched back towards the door, Mark and Sarah rushing to keep up.

"ID?" The new bouncer asked.

"Oh, I'm performing tonight. I wanted to ask if I was OK to come in the front door, or is there a stage entrance?"

The woman frowned, her lips pursing. "You were supposed to be here before six. Sam doesn't like performers walking through the bar." She continued to eye him carefully. "Fine, just this once. Get through quick. If it upsets Sam, it's on your head."

"Thanks, I owe ya." Harry replied with a cheeky smile.

The bouncer turned her gaze to Mark and Sarah, who just stood in silent disbelief.

"W-we're his... groupies – I mean, roadies." Mark stammered, an embarrassed flush creeping up his neck.

The woman looked unimpressed, but nodded to the door. "Get on with you."

Trying to appear cool and collected, as though he frequented bars weekly, Mark followed on the heels of his friends, terrified he would be thrown out again.

The interior of Peril was a clash of traditional pub and trendy, with the 'old' décor looking a little too perfect. People laughed and chatted, clustered in little groups, at tables or lounging by the bar with a natural confidence that made Mark feel young and small.

"What now?" Harry asked.

"I feel like we should be ordering gin drinks." Sarah mused, hypnotised by their hip surroundings.

"We look around, see if we can find Damian. If he's not here, we can ask around – see if anyone remembers him, and where he might have gone." Mark replied, gazing about the pub.

"Dave! Dave!" A diminutive woman with a clipboard pushed into their circle, looking up at Harry. "Dave Underhill? Missy told me you'd finally arrived – you're cutting it close! Where's your kit?"

"Sorry, I got mugged on my way here, some git nicked my guitar." Harry said, completely unfazed.

Mark bit the inside of his lip, trying to stop himself from laughing at his best friend's performance.

"Oh, you poor dear." The woman said, her comforting words slightly ruined by her manic air. "Well, you're here now. Your set is due to start in five minutes, I'm sure you can borrow a guitar off one of the others, tonight. Come on, come."

The woman grabbed his arm and dragged Harry away.

"See you later, Dave." Mark said, his voice shaking with humour. He shook his head, as his best friend got taken away. "When did he get so good at lying?"

"It's an inborn skill." Sarah said with an adoring sigh, before looping her arm around Mark's. "Come on, let's find your lover-boy."

Mark allowed Sarah to steer him to the bar area, where they asked the bored-looking bar-staff if they'd seen Damian. They dutifully looked at the photo on Mark's phone, but Mark could already tell they wouldn't help.

He sighed, and moved further back into the establishment, where people gathered in front of a stage, waiting for the next act to come on.

Mark felt a pressure on his back. He turned to see set of dark eyes boring into him. A woman sat alone at a corner table. She had dark brown hair that fell in luscious waves, around an ageless face. She was oddly familiar, though Mark was sure he'd never seen her before.

Mark's skin crawled, at her unflinching gaze. At this distance, it was impossible to tell whether her eyes were the black of a demon's; so Mark tried to read her aura. He didn't want to draw attention to himself, but Mark couldn't help gasping; the woman had no aura. Mark had never seen that – even demons had auras…

Mark's attention was dragged away by a ripple of applause, and Sarah tugged painfully at his arm.

"He's here." She hissed.

"Damian?" Mark asked, searching for his ex.

"No, Harry – look."

Mark followed Sarah's gaze to the stage, where his best friend walked on, looking more sheepish than usual.

Out of the lukewarm applause, one voice rang out. "Hey, you're not Dave!"

"That's right, I'm 'not-Dave'." Harry said, casting a nervous glance to the side of stage. "But let's see if we can do this thing…"

The first notes rang out. Mark knew that Harry could play, but when he started to sing, everything came together to give Mark chills.

The crowd went silent, completely engaged by the young gentleman on stage. His Yorkshire tones were musical and addictive.

For the next few minutes, nothing else was on Mark's mind. As the first song stopped, and the crowd applauded enthusiastically, reality came crashing back in.

"He's… really good." Mark said, his voice breaking. It was an understatement, Harry was amazing. Mark felt guilt all over again that he had failed to support his best friend at his first performance.

Harry moved onto a second song, and a third. Along with the rest of the crowd, Mark was hooked, completely forgetting their reason for coming. When Harry wrapped up his set, Mark realised that he hadn't found any clues to Damian's location.

He looked behind him, but the suspicious woman at the corner table had vanished. When he turned back, he saw Harry making his way through the crowd towards them. He got stopped along the way, by people congratulating him and even taking selfies with him.

Sarah dashed from Mark's side, leaping into Harry's arms and kissing him.

Mark wanted to welcome him back too, although in a less extreme fashion. As his friend's romantic kiss turned into a very uncomfortable public snog, Mark coughed loudly.

Sarah looked embarrassed, but Harry just grinned, still glowing from his stint on stage.

"You were great." Mark winced, realising how lame he sounded. "I mean, you were born to do this."

"Thanks, mate." Harry said, rubbing his neck awkwardly.

"Boys." Sarah sighed, laughing and kissing her boyfriend again.

"Did you find what you were looking for?" Harry asked, when he could finally peel himself away.

"Nah, I got distracted." Mark admitted.

"We might not have found Damian, but I just spotted a familiar face!" Sarah announced.

Mark followed her gaze to see somebody totally unexpected. Her normally scruffy clothes had been replaced by a brand-new jumpsuit, and shiny belt; but her dull-brown hair was still recognisably frizzy.

"Michelle!" His eyes locked onto his scary schoolmate; Mark pushed through the crowd.

When Michelle saw him, she did a double take, freezing to the spot for a moment, before she started barrelling backwards to get away.

There were shouts as drinks were spilt and people annoyed. The crowd stood firm, stubbornly refusing to budge for the rude young girl, slowing down Michelle's escape. She finally disappeared through a rear door, streetlights flashing outside.

Mark was hot on her heels, pushing through the door that said 'No Exit'. The cold air hit him, along with the reek of stale ale, and Mark nearly fell over a metal keg in his path.

He looked around, feeling a wave of relief that Michelle hadn't escaped. The yard was fully-enclosed, and she stood by a high mesh fence, her shoulders sagging.

As Harry and Sarah joined in blocking only exit, Michelle turned to face them, a snarl on her lips. "Let me past."

"Tell us where Damian is, and we'll consider it." Mark replied, crossing his arms. "Better yet, take us to him."

49

Michelle rolled her eyes. "You still don't get it, he doesn't want you."

"I want to hear it from Damian, not Robert's little groupie." Mark argued. "Take us to him… or else…"

Mark cringed at the lameness of his threat.

Unfortunately, Michelle seemed less-than-terrified by him. She gave a coarse laugh. "Yeah, or what will you do, white witch? We both know you don't have the guts to handle dark magic."

Mark hesitated, after seeing Michelle, he'd thought no further than catching her, and possibly relying on her good nature to help them… which was laughable. Mark shoved his hands deep into his pocket, his fingers tracing the small bag of herbs he'd almost forgotten he was carrying. Luka.

With a thought, he called on his protective spirit, and with a whisper Luka was there. The black and white collie appeared in the yard, looking up at Mark curiously.

"*We* might not be able to hurt you, but him?" Mark said, straight-faced. "Luka, sic."

Mark nearly held his breath, last time he tried something like this, using Luka to fend off demonic hounds, his trusty spirit had turned tail and dragged Mark away. Michelle wasn't to know that, and as Luka lowered his head, locking onto her with that fixated sheepdog stare, it was her turn to hesitate.

"You're lying." Michelle accused.

"And you're scared." Mark replied quietly. "Look, the sooner you give us a chance to speak to Damian, the sooner we're out of your life, and you can go back to whatever it is you're doing in London."

"Fine." Michelle muttered in defeat. "You talk to him, then you leave."

Mark nodded, stepping aside to let Michelle back into the pub. Knowing that he would only raise unwanted attention, he let Luka slip away.

Michelle cast a glance into the corner of the pub; Mark followed her gaze, noting that the mysterious woman had disappeared. He took a firm hold on her elbow.

"Don't even think of causing trouble." Mark warned.

"Wouldn't *dream* of it." Michelle muttered.

Chapter Six

Michelle led to an apartment block only ten minutes' walk from Peril. The area was clearly well-to-do, with brand new cars on the curb, and beautiful Georgian-styled, cream-coloured buildings as far as the eye could see.

Mark frowned as Michelle pulled out a key and let herself into the main door. She led up a wide staircase to a flat that took up the whole of the top floor. Inside, it was surprisingly elegant, and everything screamed money.

Mark realised he was gawping, and walked into the living area. This seemed like a ridiculous hide-out for a couple of teenagers.

Movement caught his eye, and Mark's heart skipped a beat when he saw Damian. Mark had played this moment over in his head so many times, he had rehearsed what he'd say, express how much Damian meant to him and how they were stronger together. All of that vanished, leaving Mark as a gormless idiot.

"Mark?"

At the sound of his name on Damian's lips, Mark closed the distance between them and kissed him.

The moment was magical and perfect, with Damian's familiar soft lips returning his kiss. It suddenly deepened, and Mark's thoughts were scattered as his boyfriend kissed him with an unusual intensity that sent his pulse racing. Damian was never this assertive, Dam-

Mark pulled away, trying to untangle himself. "Robert." He hissed.

"Now *that* is how to say hello. Michelle, take note." Robert's black eyes stayed fixed on Mark, a sly smile tilting those dangerous lips.

His smile faded, and a lost looked crossed his face. His eyes lightened, the blue bleeding back into the irises. The way he looked at Mark, with that sense of hesitation and innocence; he didn't even have to speak, for Mark to know that Damian had returned.

"Mark? What are you doing here?" He asked, then noticed the others in the room. "W-what are you all doing here?"

"We were worried about you. After all that happened, you ran." Mark said. "Your Aunt worked out that you'd gone to London so we... followed..."

Damian sighed and sat down, his head in his hand. "We've been over this, I needed to get Robert away from you."

"No, we've not been over this, because you hung up on me and refused to answer your bleedin' phone." Mark snapped. "Running away… you're literally handing your life over to that demon."

"No… he's weak… he's been weak since the battle, he can't keep control for more than a few minutes. I've been looking for a way to get rid of him for good. There are witches down here, too." Damian pleaded.

"There were witches up North, already working on your curse."

"Jeez, you guys are so lame at arguing." Michelle groaned. "I need a drink, if I need to listen to this shit."

Mark had almost forgotten she was there, and heard the clink of glass as Michelle poured some rose wine, looking perfectly comfortable in the flat. Her and Damian, in a flat alone.

"Why her?" Mark asked. "Why this place? We went to your Gran's house in Bexley, I thought you'd be there."

"You did?" Damian paused, looking touched. "The flat belongs to Robert. It seemed like a safe place to be; the downside is it comes complete with an unwanted roommate."

There was a sharp buzz that made Mark jump.

Damian sighed and walked over to the intercom.

"Damian, it's Aunt Maggie." The tinny female voice crackled through.

Mark paused, processing the impossible arrival of Damian's aunt. He glanced questioningly over at his friends.

"What, you thought we'd swan off to London, in search of a demon, without letting the adults know?" Sarah asked, crossing her arms. "We've been keeping Miss Cole informed every step of the way. She jumped on the next train down."

"What?" Mark didn't know whether to feel relieved or betrayed. It definitely put a dampener on his grand gesture.

A few moments later, Maggie and her new girlfriend, Miriam, walked through the door. The flat quickly feeling less spacious.

Maggie wrapped Damian in a fierce hug and spoke so quickly, Mark couldn't make out what she was saying. By the looks of it, Damian was getting the beration of a lifetime.

As a fellow-witch, Miriam shuffled towards Mark, looking concerned.

"You should have told us what you planned." She warned, quietly.

"Someone might have stopped us." Mark reasoned.

"Of course we would have. It took everything to stop Nanna coming." She looked Mark straight in the eye. "We're not supposed to go to London. It's too dangerous."

Mark tried not to roll his eyes. "I know there's all the stories about stabbings in the capital, but we've gone round quite safely."

"What?" It was Miriam's turn to look incredulous. "I sometimes forget how little you know. A very powerful coven is in charge of London, and they're… different from

55

us. They are mean, and territorial. Please tell me you haven't used any spells whilst you were here."

"Oh." Mark felt cold at his lack of witchy-knowledge again. "Just one location spell. Oh, and I summoned Luka – my protective spirit – but only briefly."

Miriam frowned. "Not much, you might have escaped notice. We need to get home as soon as possible."

"No arguments here." Mark glanced over at Damian – he looked in pain, and Mark hoped that his desire to stay away was collapsing. "Come on, Damian. You can see how many people care for you, and this is even without the football posse finding out you've done a runner."

"Fine! Fine, I'll come home." Damian's voice faded, along with his resistance.

"It's too late to get a train home now. Can we stay here tonight?" Aunt Maggie asked.

When Damian nodded, Mark felt a wave of relief. Now that he'd found him, Mark didn't want to let him out of his sight for a minute."

"Yay, sleepover." Michelle groaned loudly, and poured herself another glass of wine.

"Y'know, we're not actually here for you Michelle, nobody wants you to come back." Harry snapped.

The troublemaker glared at him with such hatred, Harry quickly back-tracked.

"I mean, you're free to do what you want…"

Sarah shook her head at her boyfriend's sudden lack of confidence, but didn't dare say anything to Michelle.

Later that night, when everyone was settled on every soft surface they could find, Mark lay on the double-bed next to Damian. It would have been much more romantic if Sarah wasn't on the other side of him, snoring very loudly for such a tiny person.

Damian was still awake too, and for a long time, Mark lay there staring into his clear blue eyes.

"Mark?" Damian finally whispered.

"Yes, Damian?"

"I'll come back on one condition."

"Anything."

Damian winced at his blind promise. "I'll come home, but we're not getting back together."

Mark went cold. "What?" He hissed.

"Robert's already singled you out and caused you hell. Maybe it's my fault, he knows you're my weakness. If we back off, be just friends, you might be safer."

"Damian-"

"That's my condition. Take it or leave it." Damian said, rolling over to stop any further argument.

The following morning, they were all awoken before dawn by Aunt Maggie. She had booked tickets for a ridiculously early train, clearly keen to get Damian back on route to Yorkshire, before he could change his mind.

At some point in the night, Michelle had disappeared, but no one seemed particularly concerned with finding her before they left.

Mark was happy to be heading North again, although not feeling as victorious as he would like. Everyone expected him to sit next to Damian, but with Damian's declaration last night, Mark felt an awkward barrier between them, which was tested every time the train rocked and Damian's arm brushed against his.

There was nothing Mark could do, as Harry and Sarah, and Maggie and Miriam settled into their seats as disgustingly happy couples.

Chapter Seven

Perhaps unsurprisingly, Mark was grounded. His parents had been less-than-pleased about his impromptu night out in the capital, and even worse, they'd a long time to think about his punishment. Mark had thought it was tough being grounded before, but now he was restricted to his bedroom for the rest of half-term. There would be no computer, no watching TV, and the only reading he was allowed to do was exam revision.

Mark hated that he'd upset his parents again, it had never been his intention; but these restrictions on his freedom were already grating. Each minute that dragged by was time wasted; time that Mark could spend repairing his friendship with Harry, checking on his flight-risk-ex-boyfriend, or finding out more about the new demon in his life.

Trying to counter some of the mind-numbing boredom, Mark was watching Youtube videos on his phone, the volume so low he could hardly hear it, making the usual nonsense that much harder to understand.

He was concentrating so hard in the silence of his room, that he jumped a mile when his door slammed open loudly.

"I wasn't doing owt-" He blurted out, stuffing the phone down the side of the bed, before he noticed that his intruder was Nanna. "Oh, it's only you..."

"Aye, it's only me..." Nanna replied with a shake of her head. "What the bloody hell did you think you were doing?"

Mark groaned audibly. "Seriously? I've already had a bollocking from Mum and Dad; consider me told."

"As your coven leader, I have just as much right to be angry about this." Nanna stated, struggling to keep her voice level. "You ran off without thinking – again! Don't you know how dangerous London is?"

For a moment Mark was cowed, Nanna's temper had never flared in his direction before. It was a daunting thing, but he was fed up of everyone jumping on him. "No, I don't know, because *you never told me*. You teach me these *basic* spells, and I have to suffer the snide comments of other witches, when they find out how little I know."

"I'm sorry, were y'expectin' to do advanced, life-altering magic after a whole month studying?" Nanna huffed and crossed her arms. "The others don't *mean* to belittle you, they just forget you're new."

Mark threw his head back, hitting the headboard harder than he'd planned. He winced, his anger fading. "I still don't get why Dad didn't let me start training until I was sixteen. I've missed out on so much."

"We've been over this, it was his choice. You should ask him." Nanna said, easing herself onto the foot of Mark's bed. "Anyway, as I recall, you had a very normal, enjoyable childhood. You only realised it could have been different, after your training started."

Mark went to argue, but faltered.

"I need you to describe every bit of magic you used in London." Nanna stated.

Mark wanted to roll his eyes, but obediently relayed everything that had happened. From the unconventional location spell, to Luka appearing beside him. He even drew the symbol that had burnt into the grass at the explosive end of the spell. "I thought it could be demon-related, but I've not found it in the *dictionnaire* yet."

Nanna's eyes lingered for a long time on the drawing, pain flashing across her face. "That's because it's not a demon's sign... it's that of a witch."

Mark had never seen her look so worried, so he waited patiently for Nanna to continue.

"You remember we talked about dark magic?"

"Yeah," Mark replied, with a shrug. "Powerful; addictive: stay clear."

Nanna sighed, looking uncharacteristically serious. "It also corrodes your soul. Morals, notions of right and wrong, they all get skewed, in the search of the next power fix. Dark witches will think nothing of killing innocents, and light witches. The... coven that rules London has been seduced by demon magic. You could have died, going blindly into their reach."

Mark shivered at the sudden realisation of the danger. "But... you're the Grand High Witch, can't you... do something? Order them to stop?"

"I'm a powerful witch, Mark; not bleedin' royalty." Nanna said, her usual sarcasm suddenly back. "I'm the leader of my coven, and I'm strong enough that witches from all over the North of England respect me; but I don't command anyone. London is way beyond my reach, they recognise no authority other than their own."

"So... what do we do?"

"*You* do nothing. Keep away from London, continue your training. My coven will keep an eye on the dark witches." Nanna stated, crossing her arms. "And for goodness' sake, concentrate on your schoolwork. If you don't do well in your exams, you can say goodbye to magic."

Mark didn't dare say anything, he'd already had so much taken from him; he couldn't bare losing his new life of a witch, too.

"Come on, it's time you learned how to harness the elements." Nanna announced, suddenly.

Mark followed Nanna outside, zipping up his coat against the cold. He was bored of winter, and wanted spring to finally warm things up. As keen as he was to learn a new spell, Mark wished the lesson was taking place in the comfort of Nanna's kitchen.

Predictably, Nanna went out in her favourite house cardigan, the older woman immune to the cold.

Mark bounced on the spot, partly to keep warm, but also from excitement. Harnessing the elements? He remembered the fire demon Robert had created at the Winter Solstice; and the rock monster Silvaticus had controlled only a short time ago. Now *that* was real magic, and Mark couldn't wait to replicate it.

"Magic that affects the elements should always be treated with respect. The stuff you've learnt so far, lighting candles and small spells, don't have any major consequences. Working with the real thing, is different." Nanna explained, raising her face to the cool breeze. "You can summon the wind, but for a very limited time. Too much will cause an imbalance, and the other elements can react violently, causing floods, earthquakes and firestorms."

Mark shuddered at the potential consequences. "OK, I won't push it." He said nervously.

"Don't worry, you're not powerful enough to sustain the spells to dangerous levels." Nanna replied.

Mark groaned, Nanna had a truly magical way of insulting him during her explanations. "Thanks."

"You're welcome." Nanna gave a knowing smile. "You won't always be a beginner, Mark. Plus, you're from a particularly strong witch bloodline; just give it time."

"You mean I'll become as strong as you?" He asked. Every time he witnessed his carefree Nanna as a witch, Mark was always dazzled by her power.

A shadow crossed Nanna's face. "It's not quite that straight-forward; but yes, one day you'll be one of the most powerful witches in the country. *If* we can get on with the blasted lesson…"

Mark bit back a smile; lately he'd been feeling more of a liability than a real witch. It was good to know he had a bright future. He held his hands up defensively, inviting Nanna to continue.

"Concentrate on the points."

Mark closed his eyes, following Nanna's instructions. Calling to North, South, East, and West; it came almost easily now. Mark felt the familiar calm wrap around him.

"Draw on your magic, and chant the spell."

Mark felt his power surge around, patiently waiting to be commanded.

"East wind blow;

"East wind howl.

"Bend to my will;

"I summon thee."

A sweet-scented breeze picked up, building up to gusts that tugged at his coat and hair. With a rumble, a strong wind stirred, circling Mark and Nanna. It was pure power, and it felt exhilarating.

Mark tested his control, and with a thought, it blew upwards, before rolling playfully through the afternoon air. He laughed with sheer joy.

"Enough now, lad." Nanna said, her voice breaking through his euphoria.

The connection with the element was so all-encompassing, Mark had almost forgotten she was hovering at his side.

"I release thee…" Mark said, reluctantly.

The wind shivered, and lessened, dropping back to the mild breeze that had preceded it.

Chapter Eight

The rest of half-term passed too quickly, and Mark returned to school without seeing Damian again. His aunt sent regular messages, to let Mark know that Damian hadn't fled again.

Not that Mark had seen much of anyone over the last few days, as his parents still refused to let up on the harsh grounding.

Damian hadn't been on the bus to school, having gone early for football practice, so Mark didn't see him until dinner. Damian sat with the other footballers, and made no hint of inviting Mark to join him. It was only as Mark hesitated with his tray in front of judging eyes of the other students, that Mark remembered he was the bad guy, as far as his schoolmates were concerned.

Oh yeah, with everything else that had been going Mark had forgotten the awesome turn his reputation had taken. Despite his protests, the other students still looked at him like he'd turn them into toads.

"Mark, stop being an eejit and sit down." Harry shouted from their usual table. If people hadn't been looking before, they were now.

Mark had no sooner sat down, when Sarah thrust her phone in his face.

"Look!" She insisted, absolutely beaming.

Mark obediently looked to find a paused Instagram video. He hit play, and a tinny version of Harry's music poured out. It was enough to reawaken Mark's memory of that crazy day, and he got goosebumps at the echo of Harry's playing.

"You were amazing." Mark said, turning to Harry. "If I didn't say it before, thank you for getting us into Peril. We never would have found Michelle without you."

He tried to return the phone to Sarah, but she responded by punching him and pointing to the screen.

"*Look!*" She repeated.

Mark winced, and looked again, taking in the fact that it was posted by Peril's Insta account, that – without any other name to go by, they had hilariously referred to Harry as 'Not-Dave', and finally to the tiny writing that showed it had been played over eight thousand times, and already had fifty comments.

"Wow, seriously?" Mark asked, stunned at the reaction, in just a week. "This is just Harry, right? Not all the performers?"

"Just my Harry." Sarah crooned. "He dwarfed all the other videos. I'm gonna set up Not-Dave's social media accounts, we need to hit this while it's hot."

Sarah snatched her phone back from Mark and proceeded to do so.

"Sooo… I'm your roadie, and Sarah's your manager?" Mark joked.

"I'm basically pro now." Harry replied, through a mouthful of chips.

Harry held up his hand for a high-five, and Mark quickly complied, taking it as a sign that their friendship was back on track.

"Trouble in paradise, Markie?" A familiar, cloying voice came uninvited.

"Sod off, Dean." The three of them said in unison, before bursting into laughter.

Dean huffed and walked away, heading determinedly towards the footballers' table.

*****

At the end of school, Mark made his way outside, feeling apprehensive. Normally, at this time, he'd head straight to the bus, where he'd share a short ride with Damian.

Was he still allowed to sit in his usual seat next to Damian? Would it be terribly obvious if he didn't? He really wished there was a basic guide for ex-boyfriends.

As he lingered and hung back from the crowd of students escaping, Mark noticed a single figure watching him intensely, outside the border of the school grounds. It took a few slow minutes, before he finally recognised Eadric; stumped by the modern clothes and unexpected setting.

Mark stuck his hands in his pockets and walked over to his new ally. Eadric's rugged good looks had been heightened by the fashionable grey coat, his collar turned up against the light rain.

"Eadric, what a pleasant surprise." Mark said, trying to appear cool, but aware how stupidly formal he sounded.

"Mark." Eadric nodded in greeting, his green eyes sparkling as he took in the crowds of uniformed teenagers pouring out of the official building.

Mark waited for an explanation, but when none came, he finally asked, "why are you here?"

"I wanted to see more of your world. Danny tells me so much." Eadric replied, still watching the leaving students.

"You want-" Mark paused, glancing over his shoulder at the people that were causing such interest. Surely, by now Eadric had learnt that the demon he was tracking possessed a schoolkid. No wonder he was intrigued. Mark crossed his arms. "Can you sense him?"

"No. I mean-" Eadric broke off, finally looking at Mark, as though trying to work him out. He must have realised there was no point trying to play innocent. "No, not while he slæ... *sleep*."

"Right…" Despite being allies, Mark wasn't about to hand over his ex-boyfriend to Eadric. "How did you get here?"

"Danny had t'work at scōl, I axed to see more of Tealford." He replied with a shrug.

Mark knew that Danny worked at the local college as a History teacher, but he couldn't believe that super-strict Danny would let a potential demon roam free. "And he just gave you a lift into town, and left you unsupervised?"

Eadric gave a crooked smile. "I can be very persuasive."

"I'm sure you can." Mark looked him dead in the eye. "Can I speak to Silvaticus, please? Don't even pretend he's still sleeping."

Eadric stared at him, weighing him up, then nodded. His green eyes drained to black, and Mark felt a shift in his very aura.

"Silvaticus, it's good to finally meet you." Mark eyed him carefully, "You didn't do owt serious to Danny, did you?"

"Danny has been an invaluable source of information; I would not harm him." Silvaticus intoned, his voice cool and clear, his modern English excellent. "A simple distraction spell, we'll be back before he notices we're gone."

"Do you think that's wise? Deceiving the witches that are on your side?" Mark asked.

"Ah, I'd forgotten how you humans like your little rules. I wanted to try and find Robert's host; and Eadric was keen to see the new world. He has only lived in one era, one cannot blame his excitement at seeing another."

"Look, I'm gonna be honest, I'm not about to give you Robert's host, here and now." Mark said defiantly.

"I wasn't expecting it, young man." Silvaticus narrowed his black eyes. "You are testing my reaction, to see if I'm worthy of your trust..."

Mark blushed at being caught out, but kept his arms firmly crossed. "Yes."

"You have a peculiar honesty to you, Mark." The demon replied, no sign of anger in his voice or posture. "I'm simply learning the new battleground."

"You'd do that faster, if you spoke to Danny and the witches, instead of pretending to be unconscious."

"You're not the only one establishing who to trust. I've learnt that the hard way..." Silvaticus said quietly.

"Why don't you start by sharing some information. Surely you know Robert's real name?"

"Yes, of course." Silvaticus replied.

Hope flared up in Mark's heart. "And?"

"That's not how demon-names work. Only the owner of the name can share it."

Mark rolled his eyes. "Of course..." He muttered. "I don't suppose you care to share *your* real name? It would be a great way to cement our friendship."

"We aren't at that level of trust, only Eadric knows it." Silvaticus paused, chewing over an alternative. "Mayhap you can take the first steps to friendship. Show

71

Eadric more of your town, and return him to Danny's care."

Mark checked his watch, he'd missed the school bus and his parents expected him to go straight home, as part of his grounding. Then again, they didn't get back from work 'til nearly six, and what they didn't know wouldn't hurt them. Besides, Mark found the idea of spending some time with Eadric very appealing.

*****

Mark walked into Tealford town centre with Eadric. Not that Tealford had much of a town to be the centre of; but Mark guessed that this was positively metropolitan for a man who'd come rather sharply from the 14th Century.

The walk took much longer than usual, as Eadric kept pausing to marvel at each passing car, and the kids that whizzed by on scooters. A woman with three whippets on leads walked by, chattering into her phone, whilst the dogs pulled her along. Eadric saw everything with a quiet, wide-eyed reverence.

Not sure where else to go on a miserable February afternoon, Mark headed to his favourite coffee shop.

"Denise meks hot tea. Is it tea?" Eadric asked, as he took his hot mug of latte and sniffed it curiously. "Spiced wine?"

"Not quite." Mark said, watching with amusement as his new friend took a sip and grimaced.

"Tis bitter." Eadric said, frowning over at Mark.

72

"I guess it wasn't around in the 14th Century. It's coffee, the lifeblood of the modern Brit." Mark smiled, as he sipped at his own drink. He hadn't liked coffee when he was younger, and originally only started drinking it as it was trendier than tea. Now, he quite enjoyed it, but he could sympathise with Eadric. "What did you drink?"

"Mead mostly, it tests sweet." Eadric replied, his attention caught by the other customers.

"I guess this is the modern equivalent of meeting in an alehouse." Mark mused, "Not that I could take you to an alehouse… I'm still underage and the local pubs are too scared of Nanna to let me in."

Eadric looked at him in a curious way, that made Mark blush, the red heat creeping embarrassingly up his neck.

Eadric finally glanced away, towards the people of Tealford that were milling and moving in an unhurried fashion. "This reminds me o' Market Day. Once a fēowertyne niht, we'd stop werk for market, an' always stay 'til the sun set."

"Sounds great. What did you do for work?" Mark asked.

"I werked wi' me pa as a stoneman… um, we hew stone from… *crundel*…" Eadric made a motion with his hands, as though that would explain it.

"I think that's one for Danny." Mark mumbled, embarrassed that he couldn't understand. "Your English is getting much better."

"Danny is good teacher. Denise talks lots, there is much to hear." Eadric replied modestly.

"I guess things are very different…"

"Aye. I like your food. It is easy an' very many type." Eadric tried another sip of coffee, pulling less of a face this time. "My wife, she made the best stew, but we had stew many days. It was always hard werk, to draw water, cut the wood, set the fire. Our day always werk, werk, werk. Your food is *there*, like magick."

"You're married?" Mark asked, feeling his stomach nosedive into a dark pit.

"Aye." Eadric replied. "I wer' sixtyne winters when I met Eva. She wer' the baker's daughter. I met her when they biagian my pa and me to build new mill stones. She wer' the fairest mæden I'd ever seen, and I fell for her that moment. Of course, when we went back wi' th' finished stones… I was so *unéaðnes,* I dropped them an' they break. I had to start again!"

Mark thought he'd followed the gist of Eadric's story, with only a few phrases he had to guess at. Eadric and Eva, they sounded like the perfect couple. Mark reminded himself that it was nice to find out more about Eadric's history, he had no reason to feel jealous.

"She *acwælon…* um, died… last summer." Eadric's voice broke.

Mark sat there numbly for several long moments, shocked by the announcement. "I'm so sorry." He eventually said, knowing the words wouldn't help. He reached out, placing his hand over Eadric's wrist, wishing there was a more useful expression.

"Duke Robert killed her." Eadric said quietly, leaning in, so no one else could hear.

"Robert?"

A flash of light broke Mark's focus, and he looked up to see black coattails disappearing through the door. He swore and stood up. "Stay here, please."

Mark ran outside, the cold air hitting him hard enough to remind him that he didn't have his blasted coat. "DEAN!" Mark shouted at the figure walking purposefully away.

His schoolmate stopped and turned on his heel to face Mark. A look of guilt was quickly disguised by Dean's familiar superior smirk. "Why, hello Mark. Didn't take you long to move on, did it?"

"What are you talking about? Eadric's just a friend." Mark argued, crossing his arms to keep hold of any warmth.

"Uh huh, looking pretty cosy, in a coffee shop, holding hands… a photo says a thousand words." Dean pulled his phone out, head tilting at the image. "Not bad, maybe I should be a photographer in the future."

"It's not what it looks like." Mark sighed. "Can you please just delete it? Does our friendship mean nothing?"

"Oh Markie, after all the years of insults, our friendship is a dirty rag of a thing. No, I think I'll let the social media gods decide your fate." Dean turned away, his voice ringing with glee. "See you at school."

Mark swore, dragging a hand through his hair. At best, his reputation was about to take another hit; at worst, he'd lose every chance at getting Damian back, and his parents would see proof their son was out in town, instead of in his room studying.

"Dean!" He shouted after the retreating figure, but Dean didn't turn around.

Chapter Nine

Mark was grateful that his parents had banned him from social media. The next day at school confirmed that Dean had followed through with his threat, sharing the photo of Mark on his 'date'. Mark didn't know when his love life became public interest: he'd dated Damian for a couple of months and been for *one* coffee with another guy. You couldn't get more boring... well, if you ignored the magic and demons involved.

The students all had knowing looks. Some of the girls giggled as he passed, before returning to their gossiping. Others gave him a dirty look, silently berating him for breaking the heart of their new star striker. Mark was sure they'd shared similar sentiments and more on Facebook; and despite the aching curiosity, he was glad he hadn't seen anything.

Harry and Sarah stood in an awkward silence as he approached, looking like they were ready to burst.

"I don't want to know what everyone's saying." Mark stated, before they could blurt anything out.

His comment seemed to be exactly what his friends were waiting for, and they visibly relaxed.

"So, who…?" Sarah asked, her voice trailing off, in case there were eavesdroppers.

"His name's Eadric, he's…" Mark walked into the classroom to get away from the crowded hallway. When his friends followed him, and closed the door, he continued. "He's the human host for Silvaticus, the demon we summoned, to save us from Robert…"

Following Harry's dirty look, Mark sighed. "Fine, the demon *I* summoned."

"But… how is he here?" Sarah asked.

Mark shrugged. "Silvaticus used the link somehow to bring them both forward in time. They're here to take revenge on Robert."

Harry swore loudly. "He must be bloody powerful. I stand by what I said before – don't trust him; just because you've got the same enemy, does not make him a good guy."

"Wait, you knew about this?" Sarah piped up, punching Harry's arm.

"Ow, I didn't want to worry you. I thought the witches would send the demon packing, not take him on coffee dates."

"Ugh, it wasn't a date." Mark moaned. "Eadric wanted to see some of the modern world, and we stopped off for coffee. It's not a big deal."

"Why don't you just give him Robert and get this all over and done with?" Sarah asked.

"Because, believe it or not, I'm following Harry's advice. I don't trust him." Mark said, glancing at his best friend. "He's a demon, and I don't know if he will sacrifice Damian in his bid to kill Robert. I'm gonna do my best to keep them apart, until we can figure it all out."

"OK, we'll help." Harry offered. "As long as it doesn't get life-threatening again."

Mark's answer was cut short, when the door was opened by their harassed-looking English teacher.

"You lot are keen." Mr Black remarked.

"Of course, sir. Massively keen." Mark replied flatly.

"Can't get enough of those deconstructed poems." Harry added.

Mr Black snorted at their responses and muttered something about teenagers under his breath.

The bell rang, and the rest of the class filed in. Their gazes were openly curious Mark, making no secret of their scrutiny as they passed. *'Ah yes, and here we observe the embarrassed teenage boy who was caught cheating on his boyfriend...'* David Attenborough was missing out on a treat.

"Good of you to join us, Michelle."

Mark looked up at Mr Black's sarcastic comment, surprised to see Michelle back in their classroom, after they'd left her in London.

She looked different, more mature; someone had clearly spent money on her. Gone was the frizzy hair and frayed coat, she looked sleek and sophisticated next to her schoolmates.

Mark took a moment to focus on her aura. It was still a horrid shade of brown, proving that changing appearances only fixed the issues that were skin-deep. Michelle was still the same, troubled rebel she'd been before. Honestly, Mark was surprised that her aura hadn't darkened to the same inky blackness that hovered around Robert.

Michelle must have been aware of his scrutiny, throwing him a disgusted look, before she turned to face the front of class, firmly ignoring everyone about her.

*****

Mark saw Damian in their single shared class, and again over lunch. Mark felt like he was nothing more than an observer, as his ex refused to make eye contact. Damian was surrounded by the other football players, and their popular crowd. He looked so quiet and withdrawn, Mark wanted to go talk to him, and make sure Damian wasn't planning another trip to London. At least his footie friends looked like they were trying to cheer him up.

That afternoon Mark steeled himself to finally sit next to Damian on the bus. After all, Damian had said they could be friends, and it was his duty as a friend to check how he was doing. Mark was keen to hear first-hand, if Robert had been causing any more problems, and… and he hated to admit it, but he wanted to explain about Eadric, and counter whatever gossip was going round.

Mark's master plan was ruined by Damian's absence, as the bus rolled out of the schoolgrounds without his ex-boyfriend.

Mark reluctantly headed home, but he couldn't settle. He'd gotten away with breaking the rules of his grounding yesterday. Despite the social media frenzy, his parents had no idea that Mark hadn't gone straight home, as he'd promised. Surely they wouldn't notice if he ventured out again, as long as he was back before they returned from work?

Mark had a few hours yet…

No sooner had the thought crossed his mind, than he grabbed his bike, racing over to Damian's house.

The quaint village where Damian lived with his aunt came into view, the houses sitting quietly in the bright afternoon sun.

Mark dropped his bike in the garden, and rapped on the door before he lost his nerve.

The door finally opened to reveal fellow-witch Miriam.

Mark gave her an odd look. "Are you ever not here?"

"I could ask you the same thing." Miriam huffed, "I've got more reason than you, now. Maggie's in the living room."

Mark made his way through the tiny cottage, to find Damian's aunt sitting on a sofa, working on a laptop.

She glanced up at him and frowned. "Mark… Damian's not back from footie practice yet. Is he expectin' you?"

"Um, no. I… wanted to talk to him." Mark said, lamely.

"Damian told me you guys had split up, I'm sorry." Aunt Maggie apologised. "As a serial-dumpee, I can sympathise with you."

"No, I don't… I mean-"

"Look, Mark; you were Damian's first real boyfriend, and he's really broken up that you're no longer together. I think you should give him some space." Aunt Maggie said, wisely.

"I love him…" Mark blushed as the words blurted out. "I'm going mad, not being able to talk to him."

"Oh sweetie…" Maggie broke off, as Miriam clattered about in the kitchen.

"She's making herself comfortable." Mark commented. "She'll be moving in next."

"What two consenting adults do, is none of your business, young Mark." Maggie blushed, before confessing, "Although that's not a bad idea…"

Chapter Ten

When Mark left Aunt Maggie's cottage dusk was falling, and there was still no sign of Damian. He was probably hanging out with his new football friends, and never even thought about inviting Mark.

Mark set off on his bike, and the tiny village was soon left behind. In the fading light, the country lanes were eerily quiet, Mark's breathing and the rhythmic clink of his pedals the only sound.

Mark paused, the evening was mild, and the sky clear; but swore he could see a fog rolling in. Mark sat on his bike, a chill running down his spine at how wrong it felt. He suddenly realised there wasn't a breath of wind, yet the mist was still moving towards him.

Mark sent his senses out, and was immediately struck by the darkness and pain that reverberated within the fog. With a heavy heart, he recognised the evil creatures made from misery and violence. They were snarling beasts driven by the singular desire to hunt and destroy. 'Hell beasts' Robert had called them.

"Not you again." Mark moaned, fear pricking at his senses, as he recalled how pathetic his attempts to fight these beasts were.

This time, he didn't have his panicked students screaming in the background. Instead there was an eerie silence, and an overwhelming feeling of being alone.

Mark swore and swerved away from the main road, ducking down a farm lane, and cycled like his life depended on it. If he could only get around the beasts, if only he could get to safety; then he could concentrate on what to do next.

An unearthly howl ripped through the night, and Mark knew the creatures had altered their path, as the hair raised on the back of his neck and everything screamed danger.

His bike wheel twisted as it hit a deep bit of gravel, but Mark managed to wrestle it back, his pulse pounding in his ears. A moment later, he hit a deep rut, and suddenly the world was turned upside-down.

Mark came crashing down hard on the farm track, the air knocked out of his lungs and his whole body feeling bruised. Dazed and exhausted, Mark was more than happy to stay where he was.

A cold, doggy nose nudged him, and a tongue licked at his cheek, bringing his attention back to the danger at hand.

"Luka, good boy..." Mark murmured, idly stroking the dog's ears. He pushed himself up, ignoring the aching bruises, and the sharp sting of grazed skin on his hands and face.

The hell beasts were prowling close now, Mark could see the glow of their eyes, some red, some black, some inky like the night sky.

He quickly went over his inventory of spells, which unfortunately didn't take very long. Mark had tried using Luka last time, which had been less-than-successful in repelling the beasts. He still had his barrier spell, but that wouldn't last forever, and this time he hadn't time to call for back-up. He only had one new spell...

"East wind blow..." Mark began to chant, and the still air began to shiver as his magic bled into it. "East wind howl..."

A stronger breeze pulled at his trousers, and Mark could hear an elemental roar of his own making. The hell beasts paused in their stride, heads cocked aside and ragged ears pricked.

"Bend to my will, I summon thee." Mark felt the spell lock into place, as though it were a part of him.

He sent a gale-force wind slamming into his enemies. Despite the fog that surrounded them, they were real enough, and were physically thrown backwards, tumbling undignified through the air.

Mark watched as they were forced back, beyond the edge of the field, and back into the shadow of the oncoming night.

Feeling victorious, and remembering Nanna's warning about abusing elemental magic, Mark let the spell drop.

Beside him, Luka growled, his hackles raised; and Mark watched with dismay as the hell beasts returned, the fog rolling back towards him in the darkness.

Mark's spirits fell, he'd poured so much energy into his last spell, he wasn't sure he could summon another wind, and the mere thought of conjuring a barrier made his knees shake.

"*Dī bag sage.*" A voice floated across the shadowy fields.

Mark felt the dark magic in the air, thick and oily, before it fell onto the creatures. The reaction was immediate, they crumpled, screaming in agony, before disappearing into nothingness.

Mark turned to face his rescuer, making out the blonde hair in the dying light.

"Damian?" He breathed.

Luka continued to growl, turning towards the newcomer.

"Robert." Mark said, his heart dropping. He was in no condition to fight Robert, and wanted nothing more than to be as far away from him as possible.

"Stop scowling, is that any way to greet me, after I save your life?" Robert snapped, before smiling mischievously. "You were much more welcoming last time."

Mark winced as Robert ran a suggestive finger over his bottom lip.

"I thought you were Damian, you know that." Mark argued. "And you probably conjured those creatures yourself."

"The hell beasts?" Robert raised a brow. "Not really my style. They were on my trail, though; I don't suppose you know anyone who would be desperate enough to send them to hunt me down?"

Mark didn't like the clear allegation. "Eadric wouldn't do that." He said, defending his new friend.

"No, Eadric always was a dim-witted fool. *Silvaticus*, though..."

"Why should I believe you?"

"I can't lie, it's one of the quirks of my existence." Robert said dismissively.

"Why are you here?" Mark demanded, trying to change the focus.

"You were the one who dragged me back to Yorkshire, Mark." Robert reasoned, with a distracting smile. "And I was having such fun in London. There were some deliciously dark witches that were only too willing to do... anything."

"Sorry to spoil your fun." Mark huffed, trying to move his hand without the demon noticing. If he could only get his mobile, he could call for the cavalry.

"You're getting stronger." Robert said, his eyes moving down in a way that made Mark want to squirm. "If only you'd accept my power – with dark magic you'd never have to worry about hell beasts or anything else. You'd no longer need rescuing like a damsel in distress."

"I'm not a damsel, and you're the one doing the distressing." Mark argued, his fingers closing securely around his phone. "Why do you care, anyway? It was only a few weeks ago that you tried to kill me."

"You have a funny way of recalling things, dear boy. I haven't been trying to kill you, I've been trying to unlock your potential."

A chill ran down Mark's spine, unsettled by Robert's unexpected comment. "Why?" He asked, his voice shaking.

"I like you." Robert raised a brow, daring Mark to respond.

The demon took a languid step closer, but halted, as Luka put himself in his path. The dog's growling intensified, and he shifted his balance, ready to pounce on the enemy.

"Stay away from me." Mark hissed.

Robert turned his black eyes to Luka, wariness breaking through his cocky expression. "One day…"

He vanished into the night air, leaving Mark alone.

Chapter Eleven

Mark stood numbly, going over what had happened. He'd thought Robert was the enemy and Silvaticus the hero, in this story; but now he was more confused than ever. Neither were knights in shining armour, perhaps he should have listened to Harry all along, and kept his distance from all demons. But he still loved Damian. If he had to do it all over again, he'd probably make the same choices.

The only thing Mark knew with certainty, was that he couldn't stay in this field.

He hobbled over to his discarded bike, every bit of him aching. Despite his tremendous fall, the wheel didn't look damaged, and he managed to get on and slowly ride it home, ignoring the pain that screamed in his knees.

As Mark turned up his drive, he saw his parents' cars. Wanting to put off the nightmare that was waiting for him, he made for Nanna's side of the house.

Her kitchen was warm and welcoming, as always. He took a moment to grab the jar of healing salve he'd recently made, and rubbed the pale green paste onto his various scrapes. It stung for a few moments, before soothing the pain.

The back door flung open, to reveal a very flustered-looking Nanna.

"You were right." He said, before she could lay into him. "Boys do pick up injuries like flies on-"

"Do you know how much trouble you're in, young man?" Nanna cut in.

"I can guess." Mark replied, exhausted.

"What happened?" Nanna asked. She sat next to him at the kitchen table, taking the healing paste away from him. She gently applied it to a cut on his face, and Mark could feel her feeding her magic into him. It felt electric, like pure energy; something familiar but completely overwhelming.

Mark took a few deep breaths, as he got used to the power. "Robert."

"He attacked you?" Nanna asked, worried.

"No, he… saved me. There were more hell beasts tonight."

"Really?"

"Yeah, Robert suggested that Silvaticus summoned them." Mark said. "Do you think that's possible?"

Nanna swore so loudly, it made Mark chuckle.

"You're supposed to set a good example." He reminded her.

"Utter bollocks. That's your parents' job." Nanna retorted. "Speaking of, they are furious. I'll go through first, and explain… at least some of what happened."

"OK." Mark said, grateful that Nanna would be the buffer in the true battle tonight – facing his parents after breaking their rules. Again. "What happens next with Silvaticus?"

"I'll call Denise, we'll see if she and Danny can get anything out of him." Nanna sighed and looked at Mark curiously. "If that doesn't work, maybe we'll send him your way. The host seems to like you, and Silvaticus has been more open with you, than anyone else."

"If we're relying on my ability to charm *anyone,* we're screwed." Mark commented.

"Don't worry, I'll whip up a truth potion, so you can be your usual charmless self." Nanna grinned, despite the trouble that was brewing.

"Thanks." Mark muttered, eyeing her suspiciously. "What are you so cheerful about."

"Nowt much." Nanna replied with forced airiness. "I just heard on the grapevine that my farrier is away for three months, taking part in a course in America."

"And that's a good thing?" Mark asked, not sure he was following. "I thought you liked him?"

"Of course I do, he's like Thor embodied." Nanna confirmed. "But… his uncle is covering his work here. Rosie that keeps her horses at Fir Tree, was raving about him. Supposedly, he's quite the looker."

Mark rolled his eyes, wincing as the movement caught the graze on his face. "Thanks for the warning." He couldn't help smiling, at the thought of Nanna crooning over *two* farriers for the next few months.

*****

That evening went about as well as Mark anticipated. His parents were angry that he'd left the house, when he was still grounded; but Nanna had fought his corner. In the end, Mark was sent to bed without dinner; but his Mum quickly caved, in view of his injuries, and took him a tray with stew and what looked like half a loaf of bread.

The next morning, Mark got ready for school, under the heavy glare of his Dad. Mark was getting fed up of this new normal, and he longed for their old relationship of trust.

"What?" He snapped. "What more do I have to do, to make this right?"

"You can start by keeping your promises." His Dad snapped back. The older man looked uncomfortable at his own outburst, and shook out the newspaper, turning his attention back to it.

"It's not that simple, and you know it." Mark argued. "Or you would if you took any interest in our witch heritage."

Mark froze as soon as the words left his mouth. The look of pain crossing his Dad's face was enough to make Mark regret what he'd said.

"I told you before," Dad said quietly, "just because I don't use magic, doesn't mean I'm ignorant of the witch ways."

"Why didn't you train to be a witch?" Mark asked for the umpteenth time.

His Dad folded his newspaper and got out of his armchair. "I need to get to work, and you're going to miss the bus at this rate."

"Stop deflecting, and just be honest with me." Mark argued.

His Dad's face reddened, and Mark wondered if he was going to shout, or just explode.

"I..." His Dad took a deep breath. "There was a witch that I was very close to – that went as dark as you can. To see someone you trust get seduced by something evil... it terrified the life out of me. If dark magic could change them so drastically, I didn't want to risk being tempted. Perhaps that was cowardly of me, but it was the choice I made."

"I... I didn't know." Mark said quietly, shocked by the revelation.

"It's not the sort of thing brought up in conversation." His Dad said bitterly, motioning to the door with his newspaper. "You better get to your bus. We don't want to give the school another excuse to expel you."

Without waiting for his son to respond, he promptly grabbed his car keys and left for work.

Dazed, Mark joined his fellow students on the school bus. The rhythmic rumble of the vehicle didn't help make sense of his thoughts, but it was soothing in its own way.

"…sheep. I heard half his flock was killed…"

"…awful, all torn up…"

The sound of his gossiping schoolmates caught his attention, and Mark turned in his seat, gaping at the two girls behind him.

"What was that?"

"The attack on Mrs Drew's sheep last night." One girl said.

"Nikki said it was a wolf." The other commented, her eyes glowing at the possibility.

Her friend rolled her eyes. "There's no wolves in Yorkshire. It was probably loose dogs again; remember how they harried my aunt's farm last year, and she lost a load of lambs?"

"Such a boring explanation."

The girl shrugged. "My petition to make dogs on leads mandatory has been shared a zillion times on Facebook." She glanced back at Mark. "I'm surprised you didn't see it."

"I've been… taking some time off social media…" Mark replied. At the girl's knowing smiles, he turned back to the front of the bus.

When they got to the schoolyard, Mark noticed that the dead sheep were the hot topic. He had a cold feeling he knew the real culprits; it was too much of a coincidence

94

that the hell beasts had been prowling the countryside last night.

Mark ignored the accusing glances that his schoolmates shot him, and went to find his friends.

Harry was always early on a Tuesday. Despite the fact that playing in the orchestra always wound him up, he religiously took part in practice.

Mark was surprised to see his best friend looking pleased; it was enough to make him break his stride. "Good practice?" He asked, warily.

"Nah, it were crap." Harry said, grinning. "They are really starting to take the mick on how few notes they give guitars. I don't think they'd notice if I didn't play."

"And... that makes you happy?"

"Don't be daft." Harry chuckled. "But in other news, my 'manager' has booked me a gig."

"What?" Mark asked, suddenly excited.

"Yeah, 'Not-Dave' has his first official gig in Leeds, this Saturday."

"You're kidding me! That's brilliant, I can't believe Sarah has managed to get this so quick." Mark grinned. "I'll be there. Of course, I'll be there."

"Thanks. Don't... don't tell too many people about it." Harry said, looking sheepish.

"Why? You're awesome, and I want to brag on your behalf."

Harry shrugged, "It might sound weird, but I don't mind performing in front of strangers. It's the idea of singing in front of students I have to see every day that terrifies me."

"Fair enough." Mark chewed his lip. "I'm kinda grounded at the moment, would it be OK if I bring my parents?"

Harry frowned. "Sure."

The bell rang, putting an end to their conversation.

Chapter Twelve

Mark remained on his best behaviour all week. His Mum was over the moon when she heard Harry was following his dreams; but Mark didn't put it past his parents to go to the gig without him, if he put a foot out of line.

He managed to get all the way to Saturday without any arguments, or disagreements bigger than what to have for dinner.

Nanna barged through the front door, wearing her best coat. "Let's get this show on the road. I can drive."

"No!" Everyone shouted together.

"That's OK, Nanna; Michael has already offered to drive." Mum said, sharing a conspiratorial look with Mark's Dad.

"Humph, don't know what's wrong with you." Nanna grumbled. "Denise and the others are meeting us there."

Mark stared at her. "Denise and the others?"

"Yes, I told you they were coming."

"No, you didn't." Mark argued.

"Oh, then I guess I'm telling you now. Eadric wants to see more of the modern world." Nanna pulled a small jar out of her coat pocket. "Here's the truth potion I promised."

Mark tried not to roll his eyes as he accepted it. A clear, blue-tinged liquid filled the jar.

"Now, this will only work if Eadric takes it willingly..."

"What?" Mark gasped. He couldn't imagine what would happen, if he went up to Eadric and his demon, and asked them to take a truth potion.

"It is wrong to force people to share their secrets, such magic would have a backlash." Nanna reasoned. "You'll work it out."

The venue for Harry's gig looked quite industrial from the outside, but inside it was a typical bar, with leather seats strewn across the massive floor. There was a stage, with dark grey curtains drawn across it.

It was still early in the evening, and most people were busy chatting, as rock music played in the background. Mark spotted Harry and his family, and made a beeline for his best friend.

"Hey, Not-Dave. Ready to go?" Mark asked grinning. He looked about, "Where's Sarah?"

"Oh, doing 'manager stuff'." Harry replied with a shrug. "I think she's negotiating my fee, and social media rights, or summat."

"She must be loving it." Mark smiled at the thought of Sarah being in her element.

"I think we've unleashed a monster." Harry replied, conspiratorially.

An hour or so later, Mark spotted Denise's vibrant turquoise hair. In her wake came Danny, wearing a suit and looking more out of place than the 14th Century man that accompanied them. Eadric was dressed simply in blue jeans and a loose white shirt, his shoulder-length hair fell in soft waves. Despite the simplicity, he was still the most handsome guy in the room.

As Mark headed over, there was a sudden burst of applause as the first band came on stage. The singer introduced themselves, before the band began to play indie rock.

"Enjoying yourself?" Mark asked, falling beside Eadric.

"Your ale is… nice. It doesn'y 'ave a kick, tho'." Eadric commented, sipping at his pint, before offering it to Mark. "Do you want some?"

"I'm not old enough, you have to be eighteen to drink." Mark blushed. "Not that I drink much, I prefer pop."

"Ah, I like this music." Eadric said, nodding towards the stage. "Y'friend Harry is playin' tonight, no?"

"No, I mean, yes. He's on at nine." Mark looked over to his best friend. Harry was standing with his family, and Sarah bouncing on his arm. Mark had never seen him look so happy.

Mark felt a pang on envy, at the scene. Harry had his girlfriend, proud parents, and his dreams coming true. His own life was falling apart.

"Are y'alright?" Eadric asked, his green eyes showing genuine concern.

"Yeah, I'm fine." Mark said, unconvincingly. "Do you ever think that life is just one big hurdle?"

"I ken." Eadric replied sadly.

Mark felt an embarrassed blush creep up his neck. He was such an insensitive prick, whinging about his lot in life, when Eadric's wife had been killed, he was possessed by a demon, and then been ripped out of his own time. "I'm sorry, Eadric, I wasn't thinking."

"It doesn'y matter."

Mark spotted Nanna, who was staring intently towards them. When she finally caught his eye, she gave him a subtle nod.

Mark closed his hand around the small jar in his jacket pocket, feeling suddenly nervous at what he was supposed to achieve.

"Mark?" Eadric's voice saying his name broke through his thoughts.

"Um, can we… grab a table? We need to talk." Mark asked.

"Alright." Eadric said, narrowing his bright green eyes.

Mark led away from the stage, and the crowds, to find a quiet table at the back. He sat down and pulled out the vial, putting it on the table.

"What's that?" Eadric asked, warily, staring at the object.

"It's a truth potion." Mark said, turning it in his hands, so the blue liquid shifted. "There have been some recent events, and I need to know if I can trust you."

Eadric's expression softened, and he finally sat down, across from Mark. He reached out and took the vial, the rough skin of his fingers brushing against Mark's hand.

"You cannae force trust." Eadric said, with a crooked smile.

"I know, we just… need to speed it up a bit."

"Tell you what…" Eadric placed the vial firmly in Mark's hand. "We both tek th' potion. For every question *you* answer; I answer yours."

Mark sat back, surprised by Eadric's suggestion. The challenge in his eyes was clear.

"Fine." Mark said, trying to appear cool. "I'm game if you are."

He uncapped the jar, and knocked back a healthy glug of truth potion, before he could think better of it. It tasted quite sweet, with a flavour Mark couldn't quite recognise.

Eadric smiled, gently prising the vial from Mark's hand. He raised it in toast, and downed the rest of the blue liquid.

"Why won't y' help me find Robert?" Eadric asked, leaning forward, his expression intensifying.

"I love Damian. I'm worried you'll hurt him in your bid to stop his demon." Mark stated, the truth flowing out of him easily. "Will you hurt him?"

Eadric's gaze dropped to the wooden table. "I don't want to, but I cannae promise. No one can predict th' future." Eadric reached out and grabbed Mark's hands in his. "We're not killers."

Mark pulled his hands away. "Did you summon the hell beasts last week? Because they killed."

"My turn." Eadric corrected, a little cooler. "Why did you summon a demon, rather than use dark magic?"

Mark shook his head. "Dark magic is addictive. I've already used it once, and it was an awful experience. I don't want to risk getting hooked. Now, answer my question: hell beasts?"

"No, Silvaticus didn't summon 'em. There are more demons lookin' for Robert, than ye know." Eadric leant closer. "The hell beasts are oft used as guard dogs. Some of Silvaticus' contacts are still good; we learnt that Robert was in gael."

"Demons have jails?" Mark asked, wondering what could possibly be considered bad behaviour amongst monsters. "What did he do?"

"He trapped a demon and human together an' bound 'em in eternal torture. The human cannae die, an' the demon cannae leave that body."

"That sounds awful." Mark frowned, he couldn't imagine anything worse. "Do you know who?"

"Me an' Silvaticus." Eadric went deathly pale. "It's yet to happen, in my timeline. We learnt from our contacts, what Robert had dared to do. It's why Silvaticus doesn't exist now: somewhere, we are still trapped."

"I'm so sorry." Mark said, the words feeling ridiculously deficient.

Eadric shrugged. "It's not happened yet, for me. Now I know the truth, mayhap we can change our future."

Mark sat in silence, absorbing what Eadric had told him. He was vaguely aware that, in the background there was general applause as the band made their exit, and was replaced by a couple of young women, who brought their own harmonies playing over the venue.

Recalling the setlist, Harry would be next on stage.

Eadric took a swig of beer, eyeing Mark again. "How do you plan to stop Robert, without hurting the boy?"

"Ostara is in a couple of weeks, my coven is going to channel the extra power it provides to expel the demon."

"It's a full moon, also. That may werk." Eadric mused. "Robert will be weak, Silvaticus can finally put an end to 'im."

"Without hurting Damian." Mark insisted.

"Aye. Not hurtin' your *boyfriend*." Eadric replied.

Mark sat, trying to work out his odd tone. "You said something before, about me and Damian. What did you mean?"

"I said tis agin domas… um, against *law*?"

"Great, along with witchcraft, that's two things I'd be burnt at the stake for in your era." Mark rolled his eyes. "Society has moved on."

Eadric frowned, staring firmly into his beer.

"What, didn't you have gay people in your time?" Mark asked, not sure why this wound him up.

"Aye, but it didn't matter." Eadric finally answered. "It were wrong, an' we all had a duty to our families, to marry within ye station, an' support 'em. Ye could no more court a man, than marry a princess; it is crazy."

The applause when the girls finished their act, seemed like a million miles away. Mark dragged his attention back to the busy pub, and his primary reason for being here.

"We should… I mean, I have to go up front now, to support Harry." Getting up from his seat, he met Eadric's bright green eyes. "Thank you, Eadric. I really appreciate everything you've told me."

Mark headed back to his family, who congregated close to the stage. They were all whooping and hollering like mad, when Harry made his entrance.

"Bloody hell, that's Harry!"

Mark recognised the voice, and tried not to groan. "Way to state the obvious, Dean. What are you doing here?"

"I'm here to appreciate some music." Dean stated.

"You came all the way to Leeds?" Mark asked, sceptically. "On your own?"

"Well if you must know, I came on a date, but he turned out to be a complete wet blanket. Nowhere near as hot as your date." Dean said, looking admiringly towards Eadric. "Now he is a bit of me."

"It wasn't a date." Mark retorted.

"Really? First you take him for coffee, now you two spend the last hour looking cozy at a live music event." Dean commented. "What *exactly* constitutes a date for you, Mark? You seem to be very picky."

Mark bit his tongue, trying not to let Dean wind him up any further, because playing 'truth or dare' with a demon's host wasn't his idea of a romantic evening.

At that moment, Harry began to sing, and Mark was completely distracted from everything else. His memory of Harry playing at Peril was a shadow compared to the real thing. There was a buzz through the audience, and everyone was entranced by the young man playing his guitar.

When his set finished, Mark had the awful realisation that Dean was still hovering beside him.

"Wow, he's good. Like, really good." Dean stated, looking totally amazed.

"Dean, do us a favour, don't tell everyone at school about Harry. He doesn't want them to know yet."

"OK, no need to beg. One on condition: Not-Dave plays at my next party."

"Ah, that would be Harry's call. Although you could always try his manager, Sarah."

Chapter Thirteen

Mark spent the best part of a week trying to bump into Damian in a way that he could pretend was natural. Mark couldn't tell if his ex-boyfriend was trying to avoid him, or if Damian's footie friends were teaming up to block them.

Every time Mark tried to speak with him, Damian was whisked away, with his fellow football players giving Mark dirty looks.

When Damian wasn't on the bus to school *again*, Mark decided the time for being subtle was over.

That afternoon, when school was over and the rest of the students started to make their way home, Mark headed to the football pitch. When he arrived, the team had finished their warm-up, and was moving onto training routines.

Mark sat down on one of the few benches, prepared to wait. Some of the players gave him funny looks, and the coach stared at him warily, clearly close to sending Mark packing.

Damian glanced quickly and furtively in his direction, then stayed focussed on his training. As they started to work through some set plays, Damian became totally tuned into his sport. It was hypnotic to watch him play, with flashes of grace and power, a confidence that he didn't normally have.

When practise was over, Damian grabbed his water bottle and walked over to Mark.

"Y'alright?" One of the other footballer's asked him.

When Damian nodded silently, his teammate shot a meaningful look in Mark's direction.

"If you need us, just shout."

Mark scrambled to his feet, as Damian drew near. Even though he was a sweaty mess, his ex was still ridiculously hot, and Mark felt oddly shy.

"Looks like training is coming along well." Mark said, when the silence stretched beyond awkward.

Damian shrugged, not meeting his gaze. "Everyone's still psyched after our win last term. The team is motivated and coach wants to capitalise on it. Our next game is at the weekend, we've been training every spare second."

"Oh, I guess that explains why I haven't seen you on the bus. I thought you were avoiding me."

"Well, not just that." Damian said, with a slight smile.

"I miss you." Mark blurted out. "I know you have your reasons for us not being together, but I can't begin to explain how much it hurts not getting to talk to you every day."

"Everyone thinks I dumped you, because you were cheating on me." Damian admitted, blushing bright red.

"What?"

Damian rubbed the back of his neck, a guilty expression crossing his face. "They saw the photo of you and that guy, and... I didn't correct them. I thought it was easier than admitting my demon problem. I can't lose what friends I have left."

"There's nothing going on between Eadric and me." Mark argued, embarrassed. "I mean, he's straight; and even if he was gay, we're just friends."

Damian held up his hands, defensively. "It's OK, you don't have to explain anything to me. You're entitled to be happy. I'm just sorry that I can't tell the rest of school the truth."

Damian turned away, picking up his kit bag and marching away to the changing rooms before Mark could reply.

Mark stood alone on the football pitch, a mixture of emotions clashing within him. He wished that Damian had gotten mad, that he'd raged and argued about his shitty fate, to have their relationship ruined by a demon. Mark wished that Damian had shown a hint of jealousy, that Mark might possibly move on. This quiet acceptance was driving him mad.

Mark made his way over to Denise's house, to start the official plans for Ostara. Maybe he should have told Damian about their newest plans to rid him of Robert. Or told him that Eadric wasn't competition, that he had actually been summoned from the past, and had a demon that was an ally to the witches. Or… told him how he really felt.

"*I miss you*. Pathetic." Mark groaned at his choice of words, as he marched up the long drive to Denise's house. "I love you."

That sounded better, more honest, and a much stronger argument for why they should still be together. And it was bloody terrifying. "I love you." He practised.

"I love you, too."

The voice made Mark jump out of his skin. "Bloody hell, Danny."

The boring historian got out of his car and locked it, grinning at Mark. "Who are you practising for, the old demon-possessed-boyfriend, or the new demon-possessed-boyfriend?"

"Not now, Danny. I'm not in the mood for it." Mark snapped.

"You're really going to pretend nothing is going on with you and Eadric?" Danny asked. "Even I'm not that blind."

"I'm befriending him, to see if we can trust him. That's why Nanna gave me the truth potion at the weekend."

"Truth potion?" Danny laughed, pushing open the front door to his mother's house. "No such thing, newbie."

Mark swore his heart stopped. "What?"

He marched up the steps into Denise's house. He was going to kill Nanna. And possibly Danny too, as he gloried in breaking the truth to him. Mark felt like he was going to burn up, with the embarrassment of yet another example of how little he knew about witchcraft.

"Bit hot under the collar, lad?" Denise piped up, as he walked into the kitchen.

Mark didn't say anything, just shot Nanna a dirty look, and sat as far away as possible, taking the chair beside Eadric instead.

"Nice of you to show up, Mark." Nanna remarked.

Denise flitted about, providing the newcomers with a fragrant, herbal tea.

"So, what's the big bad plan?" Mark asked.

"The coven will be gathering for the Ostara celebrations. Like the Winter Solstice, they'll stay to perform an exorcism. I think we can all agree that Damian's demon is manifested strongly enough to dispel." Nanna reeled off calmly, as though discussing the weather.

"There's also a full moon over Ostara, the timing is perfect." Denise added.

Mark waited for them to continue, but the older women seemed in no rush to discuss it further. "Is that it? It's not exactly Ocean's Eleven."

111

Nanna raised a brow, "In my experience, dealing with demons never goes to plan."

"You can say that again." Mark muttered, thinking of their failed attempt to get rid of Robert before Christmas. "Why even bother having planning meetings, if you're just gonna wing it?"

Nanna helped herself to one of Denise's lavender-infused biscuits. "I thought you might appreciate a few hours' freedom. Your parents won't argue if it's a coven emergency."

Despite still feeling annoyed over the 'truth potion' lie, Mark couldn't help smiling. Nanna was pretty cool, in her own way.

"Oh, did I tell you the news, my farrier is away for three months-" Nanna started, leaning towards Denise conspiratorially.

"Yes, you already told me. He's off to America, and his uncle is taking over temporarily." Denise finished.

Nanna looked confused, and a little upset that Denise knew the story. The expression was fleeting, and she was soon her cheerful self again.

"Well, I've got him booked to do the horses feet, so I can judge for myself how handsome he is." Nanna pulled out her phone, holding it at arm's length, and squinting. "He's coming on Thursday next week."

"Nanna, you need glasses." Mark sighed.

"I don't need glasses." Nanna argued. "Glasses are for old people."

"Rosie was still harping on about the new farrier at the bingo on Wednesday. He's made quite the impression!" Denise confirmed.

"Um, Nanna? Didn't the horses just get their shoes done a few weeks ago?" Mark asked, suspiciously.

"Yes, well, Lulu's need checking after that demon tore about the countryside without even putting her boots on." Nanna replied haughtily.

Denise chuckled, and Mark joined her.

Danny continued to sit as a permanent wet blanket.

When their gossip died down, Danny turned to Eadric. "Mark told us that you didn't send the hell beasts, but that you still have some contacts on the demon plane. Could you... find out who sent them? Get them to postpone any further attacks until after Ostara?"

Eadric nodded slowly, then looked around the cheery human table. "I'll... go outside. Ye don't want me summoning in 'ere."

The young man stood up and made his way out, leaving a cold and empty space next to Mark. He was getting used to having Eadric around, he liked his company. Mark wondered what would happen when they finished Robert's hold on Damian – would Eadric go back to his time? Or, having lost all his family, would he stay here and now?

"I've been looking into Eadric's history." Danny began, quietly. "There are various accounts of his attacks on the duke that controlled his lands. That he was strong and invincible, leading the other peasants in a revolt after his wife was killed by Duke Robert."

Mark listened to what Danny had to say. He'd already suspected as much, and he could just imagine Eadric taking up arms against an evil duke.

"After what Mark has found out, about Silvaticus being trapped within Eadric... and my own research has only made my suspicions stronger... I think Eadric has a Death Date."

Both women looked at Danny aghast.

"Oh, the poor boy." Denise said, her face pale.

"What?" Mark asked, frowning. "What's a Death Date?"

"Exactly what it sounds like." Nanna said, she chewed on her lip thoughtfully. "Eadric is fated to die, and it might not matter that he's altered his timeline."

"W-when?"

"The last reference I have of Eadric alive in the 14th Century, was Ostara in his nineteenth year." Danny replied, his professionalism wavering.

"But he's nineteen now! And Ostara is only a week away." Mark's head spun. "That can't just be it, you can't give up on him."

"We're not giving up on him, boy." Nanna snapped, "We've been in this game a lot longer than you have."

"There's a spell I can do, to confirm my suspicions." Danny added. "It will assess how fixed his fate is."

"And if it is fixed?" Mark asked.

None of the other witches met his eye.

114

"That's not fair, you can't just let him die, because fate demands it."

There was a crash beyond the kitchen. Mark's heart leapt up into his throat, and he feared how much Eadric had heard. A door slammed shut as Eadric fled outside.

Mark was on his feet, following him to the other side of the house. He joined Eadric in the garden, where Denise's fresh herbs were made pungent by the warm spring air.

"Are you alright?" Mark asked, immediately regretting his stupid question. "Actually, ignore that."

Eadric stood stock still, staring at the waxing gibbous moon, whose bright light seemed unnaturally cheerful. "I have 'til the moon is full."

"You don't know that for certain." Mark argued. "Let Danny run his tests."

"They've already accepted me fate...they're not the ones who 'ave to live it." Eadric shuddered. He looked deathly pale in the moonlight, and he sat down on the small, rustic bench. Eadric ran a hand through his long hair, twisting it through his fingers, as though ready to pull it out.

Mark sat on the bench next to Eadric, hoping his silent support would be enough.

"As far as they're concerned, I've already been dead fo' centuries. I'm expendable." Eadric's voice wavered.

"You're not expendable. Not to me."

Eadric sighed, sitting quietly for a long time. "I'm not áfærde of dying... but I am áfærde of suffering. I don't

115

want Robert to trap me an' Silvaticus in eternal torment agin."

"I won't let him hurt you." Mark swore. "You don't have to be involved with fighting Robert at Ostara. Stay away, stay safe. The witches can handle the demon."

"You have great honour." Eadric finally looked at Mark, his green eyes shimmering with unshed tears. The sight was enough to destroy Mark. "These last few weeks, I have seen so much, I've felt alive for th' first time since I lost Eva. I don't want t' die."

Before Mark could say anything, Eadric leant in. His lips were firm and demanding, his stubble grazed against the soft skin along Mark's jaw. When it became clear that Mark wasn't running away, Eadric deepened the kiss, his hands moving through Mark's hair, pulling him closer.

Mark's thoughts scattered, and all he could do was feel this man that wanted him so much it hurt. Despite his constant protests, he had fantasised about *this*, believing nothing would ever happen.

When they broke apart, they were both breathing heavily. Eadric rested his forehead against Mark's, a bitter smile crossing his lips. "I have dreamt about this, ever since you appeared to me in a vision. In my thoughts, I have sinned many times. Now, you tell me these feelings are not wrong... God, I want ye."

"Mark? It's time to go." Nanna called across the dark garden, breaking the spell.

Mark jerked guiltily away. "I should go."

"Can I see you tómorgen?"

Unable to form any more words, Mark nodded.

Mark stumbled towards the front of the house, tripping over the uneven paving slabs. His lips burnt where Eadric had kissed him. Shit, he was in trouble.

When he got into the car alone with Nanna, Mark recalled that he was still mad at her.

They travelled in silence for a few minutes, Mark looking resolutely out the window.

"OK." Nanna sighed. "What's got your knickers in a twist?"

"I'm not wearing knickers." Mark grumbled.

"I'm sorry – what has got your manly boxers in a twist?" Nanna amended, smiling at his foul mood.

"I thought we'd moved on, and I was being treated as a real witch, instead of your dumb grandson?"

"You are." Nanna glanced at him, before turning her attention back to the winding country road that was flashing past too fast. "What's this about?"

"The truth potion." Mark said dully.

"Oh, that." Nanna shrugged. "So, I told a little lie, what's the problem?"

"You're not taking me seriously. You've made me look a fool in front of Danny, *again*." Mark cringed as he recalled his questioning session with Eadric the other night. "Eadric probably knew the truth potion wasn't real, and was just humouring me."

"Eadric? Nah, that boy is even more clueless than you."

"Thanks, Nanna." Mark said bitterly. "Are you actively trying to ruin my life, or is it just a happy accident?"

"It's an inborn skill." Nanna replied flippantly, then sighed. "I'm sorry you feel bad about this, I didn't intend to disrespect you."

Mark snorted, his eyes fixed on the grey-green countryside.

"You have a lot of potential, Mark, and not just as a witch. You are an open-minded young man, who doesn't judge people by the bad decisions they make. You're loyal and trustworthy, the type of person anyone will open up to." Nanna paused. "But... you're still young and inexperienced. I can see you doubting and double-guessing your choices. I admit, I gave you a placebo, so you would learn to trust yourself."

Mark sat numbly, humbled by Nanna's comments. This was not the way he'd been expecting the conversation to go. His anger dried up in his veins, and he remained silent for the rest of the short trip.

As they pulled up to their joint house and got out of the car, Mark mumbled, "thanks, Nanna."

He rushed into his home, before this evening could overwhelm him any further.

Chapter Fourteen

Mark went to school the next day in a bit of a daze. His life was full of magic and demons, and his newest friend had travelled through time to be here; he had accepted all of these things. Now, he knew that Eadric was likely going to die, and that they had kissed last night.

Mark's dreams had been plagued by nightmares of Eadric being trapped and tortured by Robert, regardless of which route they took. In his dream mission, it didn't matter, Robert always won; and Eadric had kissed him goodbye, every time he died.

Mark was so distracted, he almost walked into Harry and Sarah. They were in a ridiculously happy mood and just laughed it off, their cheeriness clashing against the maelstrom of dark thoughts Mark was consumed with.

"What's up with you?" Harry asked.

'Deadly demons and an awkward love life,' Mark thought. "Nowt." he said out loud. "I didn't sleep well."

119

"Huh, well this news might cheer you up. Peril – y'know, the club we blagged in London – got in touch because they realised they still had to pay *me*, instead of other-Dave." Harry said, nearly vibrating with excitement. "Anyway, they were on my Insta and saw my gig in Leeds, *and* they want to invite me back *officially*!"

Mark could tell that, if Harry wasn't still trying to keep this secret from their schoolmates, he would be bouncing off the walls right now. Sarah had no such reservations, and was practically dancing next to Harry, unable to stay still.

"That's amazing!" Mark replied, genuinely pleased for him. "You deserve it!"

"So, they want me to play on Saturday night. I thought we could get an early train to London again, but this time do some proper sight-seeing first?" Harry suggested.

"Ah." Mark's stomach dropped. "I'd love to, and I know that I promised to be your roadie, but I don't know if I'll be allowed to go to London."

"Why not, your parents let you come to my gig last week." Harry asked, crestfallen. "I thought your grounding was over?"

"I think I'm technically grounded forever; but it's not my parents..." Mark took a deep breath. "Nanna has forbidden me to go to London."

"What? Why?"

"It's a witch thing." Mark tried, but he could see his excuse wasn't winning Harry over. "There are some witches in London that use dark magic. I'm not sure what they would do, if they found me on their turf, but from what Nanna said, it won't be pretty."

"A witch turf war? I didn't know that was a thing." Sarah piped up, looking more intrigued than scared.

"Neither did I." Mark shrugged.

"Well, see if Nanna will come with you, no one would dare mess with her." Harry suggested.

"Yeah." Mark hesitated. He didn't think Nanna would be able to go on a jaunt to London, so close to Ostara and disrupt all their witchy plans. "Yeah, I'll ask."

The school bell went, and Mark filed into class behind his friends.

When dinnertime rolled around, Mark was surprised to see Damian waiting for him in the food hall.

"Do you wanna grab lunch with me?" Damian asked nervously.

"Yes! I mean, yes, sure." Mark felt like a hundred eyes were burning into them, as the other students gazed towards what might be a new development for their star striker and his cheating ex.

Mark grabbed some food, without noticing what he'd picked, before following Damian outside, away from prying eyes.

Damian found a nice spot in the sports' field, and sat down in the grass, turning his face appreciatively up towards the sun. "I'd forgotten what that big yellow thing was."

Mark snorted and sat down next to him. "It doesn't rain in Yorkshire *all* the time." The spring breeze was a pleasantly-warm promise of the summer to come.

Mark sat quietly, waiting for Damian to discuss something non-weather-related. His ex looked at him a few times, and attempted to speak, getting more nervous with every fail.

Damian coughed, bright red with embarrassment. "*I missed you, too.*"

A happy warmth settled in Mark's chest, and he bit back a smile.

"I haven't stopped thinking about you." Damian confessed. "I know there's something going on with that other guy, and I want you to be happy; but I want you to be happy with me."

Mark swallowed, a pang of guilt as he recalled Eadric kissing him passionately last night. "You pushed me away, remember."

"I thought I was doing the right thing." Damian said, with a pained expression. "When we were in London, Michelle told me all about the relationship she was having with Robert. I hate that he's stolen everything from me. Not to mention that he could try to deceive you again."

Mark didn't dare meet Damian's gaze, he didn't want to tell him that he'd accidentally kissed Robert only a few weeks ago. And then there was the mysterious meeting following the hell beast attack, where's Robert's interest seemed less-than-professional.

"I told myself that you deserved someone better than me." Damian bit his lip. "But I've been stuck in a house with Aunt Maggie and her new girlfriend, watching the two of them be deliriously happy; and I've realised that I'm entitled to be happy too. I can't let the dark stuff define my life anymore. And... I'm really hoping you'll give me a second chance."

"Of course." Mark blurted out, looking at Damian's lips, bruised from his nervous chewing. "Can I kiss you?"

Damian smiled, leaning in closer. "The whole school is watching."

"I don't care." Mark closed the distance between them, finding Damian's soft lips, all of his worries evaporating.

Chapter Fifteen

Mark felt guilty that he didn't ask for Nanna's permission to visit London. Both she and Miriam had made it clear that he had to stay away from the capital. Mark didn't see the point in wasting his time asking, when he knew what the answer would be.

By the weekend, Mark's parents had eased up on their grounding, and allowed him to go back on social media. Mark browsed Facebook with a sense of detachment; after weeks of not going on, he had no idea what to post. Instagram would be no better – *here's a photo of my bedroom/prison. Again.*

Mark sighed, and tried not to feel too bitter at all the photos pinging up on his timeline, of Harry and Sarah, grinning madly in front of various famous London landmarks. The sun was shining on the young couple, as they shared their adventure with the online world.

As the afternoon crawled by. Mark went downstairs to make a cup of tea, to break up the boredom. His parents piped up with their orders, making Mark mutter under his breath about slavery.

There was a knock on the window, making Mark jump. Damian was hovering outside, biting back a smile at Mark's reaction.

"Damian, what are you doing here?" Mark asked, opening the back door.

"I biked over." He explained. "I thought if I just turned up, there'd be less chance of you or your parents turning me away."

"Why would we do that?" Mark asked, dragging him inside.

Damian shrugged, looking sheepish. "Dunno, I had it in my head you all still resented me."

"Don't be daft, come on through."

Mark led into the living room where his parents were watching a thrilling documentary on the history of Brexit. They both looked up at the newcomer, and after a moment's hesitation Mark's Mum jumped up from the sofa.

"Damian, what a pleasant surprise!" Before the lad could react, she wrapped him in a fierce bear hug.

The hug went on longer than necessary.

"Mum, you can let him go now." Mark instructed.

Mum released Damian from her hold, taking a moment to affectionately straighten his creased shirt.

125

"It's so good to see you, sweetie. Does this mean you're back together?"

"Mum!"

"Sorry." She piped up, not sounding sorry at all. "You wouldn't believe how much Mark moped around after you broke up. Such a grouchy-"

"Mum!" Mark grabbed Damian's arm and steered him upstairs, away from the embarrassing adults.

Mark perched on his bed, nervous all over again, to have Damian in his room. "Sorry about Mum."

"No, it's OK." Damian replied, hovering near the window. "It's nice… I have this whole Northern clan, where people consider me part of their family. I didn't think I'd feel that way again, after my parents died."

"Well, that's even more reason to stick around now." Mark said. "Have you told you aunt about the demon yet?"

"No." Damian didn't meet his eye. "Aunt Maggie has enough to deal with right now. Did you know, she asked me how I'd feel about Miriam moving in. Like, officially. I can't remember the last time she wasn't at the cottage."

"Wow, that's a big step. How *do* you feel?"

Damian shrugged. "It's fine, I want her to be happy."

"But?"

"I know this sounds really selfish, but I'd gotten used to it being just me and Aunt Maggie. I don't want it to change."

126

"Fair enough." Mark could sympathise with that. "But just think if this gets any more serious, you'll get another auntie in that new family you were raving about."

"Huh, I hadn't considered that."

"Enough with the serious stuff." Mark announced. "Pick a film and we'll Netflix an' chill."

Damian dropped onto the bed next to Mark, making himself comfortable. "Y'know what that phrase means, don't you?"

"Erm… watch a film and veg out?" Mark said, already knowing he was wrong.

Damian bit his lip nervously. "That's right, except it suggests sex."

Mark's blush set his neck on fire. More evidence of his bleedin' inexperience and naivety. "B-but Harry says it all the time… oh."

"OK, can we please move the topic away from the possibility your best friend is having sex?" Damian suggested. "I mean… we can talk about sex… but, um. I don't think I'm… like, ready?"

Mark was relieved to see that Damian was blushing just as fiercely, his boyfriend stumbling over his words in embarrassment.

"No. Me neither." Mark was quick to add.

"I mean, I realise things might be different now… you've been with that other guy, whose older and more experienced…" Damian babbled on.

"He's definitely older." Mark murmured, thinking how Eadric was nineteen, which qualified as more

127

mature. Technically, he was seven centuries old. "But it's not like that, we're not *together* together..."

Mark trailed off, he didn't really want to explain to Damian what had happened. He didn't want to admit that, even when they were still together, he'd been dreaming about the mysterious Eadric. It felt like cheating.

"Oh," Damian replied, slightly mollified. "So... Netflix?"

It felt nice, sitting next to Damian, leaning against his shoulder, his warmth radiating through.

Mark kept checking on social media for updates on Harry and Sarah. A little before six in the evening, they posted a picture of themselves outside Peril, and another with Harry next to one of their posters announcing 'not-Dave' playing tonight.

Later, Sarah posted photos of the other artists, and eventually a video of Harry's performance.

Mark and Damian sat huddled around his phone, the tinny effect barely detracting from the quality of music.

"He's really good." Damian said, when one song ended, and applause made the speakers crackle.

Another song started, and they fell into silent appreciation again.

Mark was so proud of Harry, getting out there and chasing his dreams. Mark sat there, still in awe of how talented his best friend was.

It was getting late when there was a knock at his bedroom door. Mark assumed it must be one of his parents telling him it was time for Damian to go home. It had been a perfect evening, and it inevitably had to come to an end.

True enough, his Dad stood on the other side of the door, but he had different news to bring.

"Mark, Eadric is downstairs."

Mark felt Damian freeze beside him, or maybe it was his own muscles locking in panic.

"OK." Mark shuffled awkwardly off the bed, looking apologetically to Damian. "I'll be back in a bit. Watch what you want on TV."

Mark made his way down the stairs, no idea what to expect.

Eadric was sitting in the cozy living room, sitting next to his Mum on the sofa.

His Mum was looking at the young man curiously, but Eadric sat with his usual reserve.

"Eadric…" Mark greeted.

"Mark…" Eadric echoed.

Knowing this was going to be awkward enough, without his parents gawking, and Damian within earshot upstairs; Mark led outside.

The night was mild, smelling of the night-blooming jasmine in Nanna's garden.

"What are you doing here?" Mark asked.

"I wanted to see you." Eadric said.

"Look, this isn't a good time-"

"I wanted to say sāriġ... um, *sorry*." Eadric cut in. "If I only have a few days to live, I want t' say sorry for kissing ye. I assumed ye liked me, also. I got carried away."

"Don't say that, we're going to find a way to stop fate."

Eadric gave a crooked smile, lacking confidence in Mark's statement.

"You weren't wrong." Mark finally confessed, quietly. "I do like you... more than I should."

Eadric's smile became more authentic, and he took a step closer.

Mark felt a familiar tension rise between them, as he recalled the passionate kiss they'd shared. It had been fierce and demanding, and made Mark's knees weak at the mere memory.

Mark put his hand up, resting it on Eadric's solid chest. "Stop."

Eadric looked confused.

"I can't..."

Mark's words were cut short by his ringing phone. Swearing beneath his breath, he saw Harry's name flash up. His best friend probably wanted to check Mark had seen his set.

Still feeling guilty about missing the trip to London, and... if he was being honest with himself, eager to delay the rest of his conversation with Eadric; Mark accepted the Facetime call.

"Sorry, I've gotta take this." Mark apologised, looking down at his phone.

He froze as an unknown woman appeared on his screen. She looked to be in her forties, but her skin was unnaturally clear of lines. Her dark brown hair fell in styled waves around her face.

"Where's Harry?" Mark asked.

"Are you Mark?" The woman countered with her own question.

"Yes, now where's Harry? What are you doing with his phone?" Mark looked into her brown eyes and felt a jolt of recognition. "Hey, I saw you in Peril last month."

"Aren't you a clever boy." The woman sneered. "If you were real clever, you would have come to London with your buddies, and I wouldn't have to take these extreme measures."

"W-what are you talking about?" Mark asked, a chill running down his spine.

"I wanted *you*, not this Ed Sheeran wannabe. It never occurred to me that you would refuse to support your best friend, when you're supposed to be one of those pathetic goodie-two-shoes white witches..." The woman sighed. "Never mind. I had to work with what I got."

The scene turned upside down, as the phone was turned away from the woman's gloating face. Once the phone steadied again, Mark could make out Harry and Sarah, kneeling on a hard floor. White material was stuffed into their mouths, gagging them from speaking; and from their awkward, strained positions, Mark

131

guessed their arms were bound. Both of his friends were red-faced, looking murderously towards their captor.

The phone shifted again, and the woman reappeared on the screen. "It's the first night of the full moon, and my coven needs sacrifices. I understand you have a demon by the name Silvaticus... I want the two of you here by midnight, or your friends will take your place."

"What?" Mark gasped, feeling light-headed. "You can't be serious."

"You're wasting my time, boy. Go to Peril, my associate will meet you there." The woman said. "If you do not come, your friends die. If you bring any of your coven, your friends die. If you do not bring the demon... well, you get the gist. You have 'til midnight."

The call ended, leaving Mark reeling. This could not be real. He was waiting for Harry to call him back and confirm it was all a prank.

"I'll go with ye." Eadric said, breaking into the silence. He looked deathly pale, his thoughts ahead of Mark's, accepting his fate.

"No, you're going nowhere near that crazy witch." Mark argued. "Midnight... none of us are... it's impossible..."

Mark checked his watch, it was nearly ten. The next train from Tealford wouldn't be until morning. Even if Nanna drove down in her usual manic manner, it could take four hours to get to London.

"Tek th' ley." Eadric suggested. "The demon road."

"What?"

"Th' ley." Eadric repeated. "Th' line of power. Silvaticus can take ye."

"Ley lines?" Mark asked, disbelieving. Demons using ley lines for transport was a stretch too far for him right now.

"Aye."

Mark looked at Eadric, his green eyes were sharp with determination, but they'd lost their brightness.

"Eadric, go home. I'm not going to put you in harm's way."

"Ye risk yer friends' lives..."

"I know, but they're already stuck in the middle of this. I'll feel guilty later, when I've got them out." Mark argued. "I'm not putting you at risk, too. Go home, go back to Denise's until Ostara is over and fate forgets about you."

Eadric stood, uncertain.

"GO!" Mark shouted, frustrated at his stubbornness. Couldn't Eadric see Mark was trying to keep him alive? That he was no use, if he threw his life away, because of some stupid witch fight?

Eadric leant back on his heels, his expression cooling. He looked like he would speak, but turned and walked away, without another word.

Mark watched until Eadric disappeared completely into the night. He wanted to call after him, he wanted an ally, he wanted *Eadric*.

Chapter Sixteen

Mark sighed and turned back to his house. He rushed through the living room, before his parents could interrogate him, then paused at the foot of the stairs.

Damian was waiting upstairs for him, probably thinking that Mark was having a lover's spat with his new fella. The truth was a little darker. The dark witch had given him until midnight, and Mark had believed her threat. If only there was another demon on their side...

Mark groaned, as a very terrible idea lodged in his head, and kicked for attention.

He made his way back to his room, heavy-footed.

Damian's head snapped up at his return, a guilty look crossing his face.

Mark noticed the curtains were now open, so Damian could see his competition, even if he couldn't hear them. Mark found it amusing, and if he was honest, a little bit gratifying that his no-longer-ex-boyfriend should be jealous.

"I have something to tell you about Eadric..." Mark confessed.

Before he could lose confidence, Mark told Damian as much as he could about Eadric, the truth about where and *when* he was from. The fact that he carried a demon, and that Silvaticus had been the one to defeat Robert last month. He neatly missed out their shared kiss, Mark didn't think Damian needed to know that.

Damian's expression grew grave. "I never thought... there's someone else like me?"

"Yes." Mark replied, "Although he has a mutual understanding with his demon. They work together. I can't imagine Robert doing that with any of his hosts."

Damian sat quietly on the bed, processing this information.

"Things have gone a little insane tonight." Mark said, not daring to look at Damian. "After I came to London to find you, I learnt there are dark witches ruling over the capital, and... it appears that I've caught their attention. They've kidnapped Harry and Sarah..."

"What!"

Mark hushed him, not wanting to alert his parents to the problem hanging over their heads. "I have to get there before midnight, otherwise..." Mark's throat closed up, unable to say the words.

"What can we do?" Damian asked, his hand gripping Mark's arm.

"Eadric mentioned a 'demon road', that demons can travel." Mark hesitated. "Robert told me that he knew some dark witches. If he can get me to London via that road, there's a chance he'll know the witches, and can stop this from getting crazy. Or... crazier..."

"Robert?" Damian looked disgusted. "Why do you think he'll help you?"

The night of the hell beast attack sprang to mind, when Robert had rescued Mark. He wasn't about to admit what Robert had said. "I don't have any other choice. If I take Eadric and Silvaticus, we'll be stepping right into the dark witch's trap. I know that I'm asking a lot, dragging you into trouble, but please..."

Damian bit his lip, but eventually nodded. His bright blue eyes fixed on Mark, trustingly. "What do I need to do?"

"Let Robert take over." Mark couldn't believe he was suggesting it.

Damian took a deep breath, and leant back against the headboard. Mark knew it had worked, as Damian's nervous ticks faded, and his shoulders relaxed. Finally, he opened his eyes, to show the tell-tale black irises of the demon.

"Robert?"

Robert took in his surroundings and smirked. "Straight to the bedroom. I do like your efficiency."

Mark jumped off his bed, as though burned. "I need your help." He said, business-like.

136

Robert rolled his eyes. "Again? You do attract trouble, Mark."

"You said that you knew dark witches in London. Do you know the main coven well enough to negotiate with them?" Mark asked, keeping the conversation on track.

"I do…" Robert replied, looking at Mark curiously.

Mark's pulse raced, "And can you use the demon road to get us to London before midnight?"

"I can." Robert said quietly. "Whether I will, is another matter."

"What do you want?" Mark's hope faltered. "You don't get to keep Damian as a host."

"We'll see about that." Robert leant closer to Mark, the bed creaking beneath him. "You will owe me a favour."

Mark shook his head. "Too vague."

"That's my price." Robert replied with a teasing smile.

Mark glanced at the clock beside the bed. Nearly half past ten, time was running out for Harry and Sarah.

"Tick tock, Mark." Robert goaded.

"Done." Mark said, knowing he would regret it. He held out his hand to shake on it.

"How very quaint. We could kiss to seal the deal?" Robert laughed at his reaction, then took his hand firmly. "Boring handshake it is."

Mark had forgotten the dark energy that brewed with Robert, and how it licked across his skin every time they touched. He snatched his hand away. "Where is this demon road?"

"Ley lines are interesting things, they connect points of power geographically, but they're not solid lines that are always in the same place. They're like rivers and waterways, which grow or disappear for a multitude of reasons." Robert nodded to the dark window, where the moonlight glowed brightly. "Normally, your nearest one is a couple of miles to the north, but tonight's a full moon, causing the lines to be super-charged. I just need to be outside to access them."

"Fine, let's go." Mark said, grabbing his coat. He paused at his bedroom door. "My parents are off limits. You are not to say *anything* to them."

Mark didn't know if his parents would realise the demon was in control, instead of Damian. It was safer if they didn't know about this.

"You do spoil all of my fun, Mark." Robert raised his hands defensively. "Fine, I will be on my best behaviour. Demon's honour."

Swearing beneath his breath, Mark made his way as silently as possible down the wooden staircase, dodging all the creaks he knew by heart. Robert glided behind him, as quiet as a ghost.

Making his way out of the front door, Mark released a breath he didn't know he was holding. "What now?"

"This may be a little bit of a light show for any observers, we may wish to move away from your house."

Mark started to walk through the garden, climbing over the low stone wall at the end, and making his way up to the same field they'd had the bonfire at the Winter Solstice. Knowing this was the scene of his first fight with Robert, Mark kept glancing over his shoulder at the demon, feeling increasingly vulnerable the further they went.

Robert seemed completely relaxed, and eventually called out to Mark. "Are we going to walk the whole way to London?"

Mark blushed, hating how the demon embarrassed him at every chance. "What do I need to do? Is there a chant?"

"It takes demon magic to access the demon road, I can tell you the spell, if you would like to use it." Robert smirked. "No, I didn't think so. Leave the tainted magic to me, dear Mark. You need to hold my arm."

"I don't think so." Mark replied, looking at Robert's extended arm as though it would poison him.

"I need skin-to-skin contact to take you with me. I was going to suggest stripping naked and dancing the rumba, but I get the feeling you wouldn't approve."

Mark's blush increased, creeping up his neck. He grabbed Robert's arm before the demon could wind him up any further; the electric current of dark magic reacting to his touch again.

Robert smiled mischievously. "*Sipwegas*." He hissed, before Mark could rethink the situation.

There was a flash of blinding, white light, followed by a dark red nothingness. There was no sound, no smell, just an odd warmth. Mark blinked away the spots of light, but it didn't help him see anything on the demon road. There was just him and Robert on this strange plane.

It dragged on for what felt like an eternity, and Mark felt his panic rising at the claustrophobic existence.

Eventually, there was an equally blinding flash of light, and the sound of a city came crashing down on Mark's senses. He stumbled at the suddenly overwhelming stimuli.

Robert had brought them out in an alley, with no witnesses to their magical appearance. All around them, there was the sound of people talking and laughing on a Saturday night, and the constant rumble of vehicles, even this late, the capital's roads still busy.

Mark felt like he had whiplash, going from a silent field in Yorkshire, to a busy London hub. Was it possible, to get magical whiplash?

Robert stood calmly next to him, straightening the cuffs on his sleeves. "I do like your boyfriends' taste in clothes. I once had a host that was dreadful, it was embarrassing every time I took over *his* body." He said, as though all of this was everyday occurrences.

"That road was bloody awful." Mark said, when he was sure he wasn't going to throw up.

"There's always a compromise, a price to pay." Robert mused. "Now, where do we meet your dark witch?"

"Peril. It's a club in Covent Garden."

Robert looked amused. "I'm familiar with it, let's go."

Without waiting for Mark, he stepped out of the safety of the alley, and out towards the main street. Robert jogged up some steps to the nearest bridge, and led the way across.

Mark hurried to keep up, not trusting Robert to stick to his deal.

Mark was surprised that the streets of London weren't as busy as a night out in Leeds. People seemed to cluster in hot spots, allowing Mark and Robert to pass unnoticed, looking like just another young couple out for a few drinks.

Mark vaguely recognised Covent Garden when they got close, and soon enough he spotted Peril. The same doorman that had refused them entry last month was standing with a bored expression.

Mark felt nervous, that this guy might be a hurdle that could cost Harry and Sarah their lives.

Robert strode up, and the bouncer looked at him in recognition.

Robert smiled and put a possessive arm round Mark's shoulders. "He's with me."

"I'm not *with* him." Mark protested.

The doorman ignored him, his gaze fixed fearfully on Robert. "Yes, sir." He stepped aside, letting them both pass.

Puzzling over the man's reaction, Mark followed Robert into the dimly-lit pub. Unlike last time, it was much quieter. The live music had ended, and there were only a few people left drinking in the dark.

Robert led up to the bar, and ordered a couple of drinks.

The barmaid blushed nervously, the drink spilling on the counter slightly as she rushed to get them out. "On the house, sir."

Robert handed Mark a drink, which he looked at suspiciously.

"What's that all about?" He demanded.

"It's called a Martini. It's not poisoned." Robert said, sipping his to make a point.

"I don't drink." Mark snapped, "And I meant why is everyone treating you…"

"Oh, like I own the place and could get them fired?" Robert translated. "Because I own the place."

"What?"

"I bought it about fifty years ago, before I was thrown in gael. I was intrigued to see how the old place was doing." He looked around at the hip décor. "I think the current manager has done a marvellous job with it."

"You own…" Mark's voice trailed off. He'd no idea. It seemed like an odd coincidence. Although, it kinda explained why they had tracked 'Damian' to Peril last month.

His thoughts were interrupted by the sudden appearance of a young man, who stood expectantly before them. He was short and skinny, but Mark could feel power radiating off the stranger.

"Where are my friends?" Mark demanded.

"Come with me." The man ordered.

Glancing towards Robert, to make sure he was still on board, Mark followed the stranger.

Robert finished his drink, setting the glass calmly on the side, before casually falling into stride beside Mark. "And so it begins." He murmured, smiling in anticipation.

Mark had the same thought, but it didn't cause any amusement, just increased nausea.

Chapter Seventeen

They walked some distance, down unfamiliar roads. Eventually, the young man leading them to their doom stopped at a wooden gate. The wall stretched high and gave no indication of what was within, but when the gate opened, Mark could sense a barrier hovering in the air, invisible to the normal Londoners.

Their guide, and Robert, both walked through without hesitation. Mark wasn't so brave, pausing for a few long moments. With no other option, he held his breath and dived through.

The barrier trickled over him, making his skin crawl at the unknown magic. Other than that, it didn't seem to have any effect. Mark surreptitiously drew on his own magic, it was sluggish and reluctant to answer his call. He tried to stamp down the rush of panic, it wouldn't do to appear weak in front of these dark witches.

They walked through a paved yard, with buildings clustered close together, much like everywhere else in London. Their guide knocked on a door, before leading inside.

In the room, the dark witch who'd called him from Harry's phone sat at a desk, scribbling busily. She barely glanced up at their entrance; but waved dismissively.

The young male witch bowed his head and backed away, closing the door firmly behind him.

Despite the fact that Mark and Robert now outnumbered this lone witch, she looked perfectly at ease. Mark guessed they were not truly alone, and her dark coven was close at hand.

Finally, she looked up, her calm brown eyes settling on Robert with no surprise, before she glanced to Mark. "So... you're the Grand High Witch's heir?" She sneered. "I expected someone... well, more impressive."

Mark ignored her jibe, not wanting her to realise he had no idea what she was talking about. "Where's Harry and Sarah?"

"Where's Silvaticus?" The witch asked, her eyes moving back to the demon at Mark's side. "As you only brought half of the exchange, perhaps I should only give you half in return. Would you like your friends' top halves or bottom?"

Mark's confidence wavered. The dark witch had been intimidating enough over the phone; in reality, she was a force to be reckoned with. Magic hovered around

145

her, and something about its oily nature sent a clear warning of how dangerous she was.

"Why do you even want with Silvaticus?" Mark demanded, trying to at least appear in control.

"He was part of a deal." She said, looking accusingly at Mark's companion. "Isn't that right, Robert?"

"Edith, you have no appreciation for drama." Robert replied.

Mark's heart stopped. Robert was in *league* with the dark witch?

The dark witch, Edith, snorted. "You didn't think he was *helping* you, boy? This demon will only do things that benefit *him*, that's the only thing you can actually trust him on."

She looked at Robert, who appeared quite flattered by her assessment.

"Did everything go to plan?"

"Perfectly, darling." Robert said with a seductive smile. "I brought you Mark, completing my end of the bargain. Soon Silvaticus will follow, which completes your side of the deal. Silvaticus' human host is besotted with this boy; he won't stay away." Robert glanced at Mark, a disdainful expression of disgust, betraying his thoughts on the relationship between Eadric and Mark.

"Why?" Mark asked, "*Why?*"

Edith turned on Mark with a blazing fury, the magic that sat idly, now rushed through her and threw Mark back against the wall. An invisible force clamped round his chest as shoulders, dangling him uselessly, as the

146

pressure increased around his throat, making it hard for Mark to breath. "Because I will have my revenge on your so-called Grand High Witch. I will take away that which is most dear to her, and turn her legacy into dust."

"Edith, you can't kill him yet." Robert said, in a bored voice.

Mark felt the spell lessen, and the magic reluctantly let him fall to the floor in an ungainly heap. In his dazed state, he tried to call on Luka, but the spell slipped from his grasp, refusing to obey. Mark felt the panic really start to rise when he realised he wouldn't even have his spirit animal's protection. He was in this alone.

"I would have killed you last month, when you stumbled into my territory. Lykaois was supposed to drug you, to bind your powers, but the stupid herb witch couldn't even do that. I tracked you to Peril to kill you, but then I found your powers fully-functional." Edith looked down at Mark with a sneer. "If I knew how pathetic you were, I would've snuffed you out then and there."

Mark stayed on the floor, a shiver running through his spine. Mr and Mrs Lykaois had seemed so genuine, he couldn't believe they would betray him. Then Mark remembered the meal they'd shared with the parents of Damian's best friend; the unusual herbs that had caught his attention and killed his appetite.

"Why do you hate Nanna so much?" Mark gasped.

"Ah yes, you lot think she's a saint. Bloody narrow-minded witches, blinded by tradition." Edith spoke calmly enough, but Mark could feel her anger vibrate through the air. "Maybe I should send a message to your precious Grand High Witch, weave your entrails into the night sky and turn the rain red with your blood."

A moment after her spell hit, Mark curled into a tight ball as pain spasmed through every inch of him. In an effort to stop from screaming, he grit his teeth so hard he was afraid he'd break his jaw.

The pain stopped as suddenly as it started. Mark tasted something metallic on his tongue, and spat out blood, which was starkly red against the grey concrete floor. He wearily raised his head enough to see Robert kiss Edith's shoulder affectionately, as he moved over to her side.

"Don't kill him too quickly, darling. I need him as bait." Robert reminded her.

Edith stared at the demon that dared interrupt her. Her magic wavered as she considered his request.

"Take him away." Edith eventually said, raising her voice.

A couple of her coven members entered the room and obediently dragged Mark to his feet.

"Wait, what about my friends, you have to release them." Mark pleaded. "You have me now."

"I don't have to do anything." Edith frowned. "This isn't going to be you or them; it's who dies first and second."

"B-but our deal."

Edith laughed, as Mark realised his naivety. The dark witch and her coven didn't play by any rules Mark could understand.

As the witches pulled him away, Mark glanced at Edith and Robert. The demon looked at the dark witch in a dangerous way, that made Mark shudder.

Mark was thrown into a bare concrete room, lit by a single industrial bulb that cast an ugly yellow light. The small, high window was barred; as was the door.

As his guards moved away, Mark recognised one of them.

"Michelle?" He stared stupidly at her, not sure if he was happy or terrified that she was here. "Ugh, why am I not surprised you're a part of this crazy coven. I didn't even know you were a witch."

Michelle glared at him with narrow eyes, as she locked the door.

"Please, you have to help me. Or at least help Harry and Sarah escape. They don't deserve whatever Edith has planned." Mark begged.

"Why would I help you? The last time you were in London, you were all more than happy to leave me behind, to fend for myself. Like everyone else in my life." Michelle sneered. "At least now I have a family, one that Robert found for me."

A wave of guilt washed over Mark. Despite Nanna's suggestion that he be nice to this troubled girl, he hadn't made any real effort. And when Aunt Maggie organised their trip back to Yorkshire, Mark confessed that he hadn't given Michelle a second thought.

Out of curiosity, Mark focussed on Michelle's aura. It was still a dirty brown that pulsed and shifted, never settling. She'd had the new clothes and makeover, and now she had a 'family'; but the truth was that it still didn't fix Michelle's real issues. She couldn't be truly happy.

"I'm sorry." Mark eventually said.

Michelle huffed and stormed away.

Chapter Eighteen

Mark lay on the cold concrete floor. The spell Edith had put on him still echoed, the pain still there, long after the magic had faded. The way Mark had convulsed, pain tearing through him... it reminded him of the dark magic he had naively used against the hell beasts that threatened Dean's party. Now he knew how they'd felt, and that no one deserved this.

"Are you still alive?"

A familiar voice from the other side of the door broke through Mark's thoughts. "What do you want, Michelle?"

There was a prolonged silence, and Mark wondered if she'd wandered off again.

"I told Harry and Sarah that you came to rescue them, but you screwed up and now you're all in trouble."

"What?" Mark groaned, pushing himself up into a sitting position. "That's hardly comforting."

"I told them you came for them, you ungrateful little git." Michelle hissed at him.

Mark sat staring at the door, seeing it from Michelle's perspective – no one ever came for her. "I'm sorry, Michelle. Thank you."

It fell silent on the other side of the door. Mark would've assumed Michelle had stalked off again, but he hadn't heard any footsteps.

"D'you know why they're so desperate to have Silvaticus?" Mark eventually asked.

Michelle sighed audibly. "That was Robert's price."

"Yeah, I get that; but why doesn't Robert just fight him, why go through this whole convoluted mess?" Mark pressed.

"Uh, because Silvaticus is *stronger* than Robert." Michelle replied patronisingly. "You remember their big clash last month, and that was just with Silvaticus being invoked by you. Now, he's fully on this plane, and even stronger. Robert has never faced Silvaticus head-on."

Mark rested his head against the cool wall. He still had nightmares about being trapped underground by the scary Robert; and being saved by the even-scarier Silvaticus. The sight of the rock monster Silvaticus created still seemed unreal.

"But my Robert is smarter than your Silvaticus." Michelle said, almost smugly. "He plans for everything. He is cunning and brutal, and will always come out on top."

Mark wished he could shut her up. Even though he saw them as two very different identities, it was still uncomfortable to hear Michelle swooning over the demon that possessed Mark's boyfriend.

"Will you help me get out of here?" Mark asked quietly.

"Go against Edith? You're bloody mad." Michelle snorted. "I hate you, but that doesn't mean I want anyone dead... there's no going against her, there's no escape from her."

"Nanna can protect you, once we get up North."

"Sure she can..." Michelle replied, unimpressed. "Your precious Nanna can't do shit in Edith's territory."

"Will you at least help Harry and Sarah? They don't deserve to be in the middle of this."

"When does anyone ever deserve anythin'." Michelle grumbled. "I best go, before I get accused of fraternising with the enemy."

Time went slowly for Mark. After Michelle left, there was barely a moment he was left alone. Edith's dark coven members came to peer into his prison, gawking at him like a strange new addition at a zoo: *here sits the grandson of the most powerful witch in the country.*

They seemed to find it very amusing, how pathetic he was, how he wasn't even a real witch... Mark heard all the jibes, as well as the dark witches congratulating themselves, for their leader was about to make a proud statement for their coven. Mark knew what that statement would be, his blood falling like rain. He had to admit that Edith had made it all sound poetic; between that and the addiction to demon magic, no wonder her coven were enamoured of her.

There was less than half an hour left until midnight. Mark tried to draw on his magic again, but still found himself stumped. Maybe when midnight came, the natural boost to his magic would overcome whatever spell blocked them. It wasn't much, but it was the only hope Mark could cling to.

He had no allies, having pushed away Eadric, and stupidly putting his trust in Robert. Mark was alone.

There were footsteps, as more people came. More gawkers, Mark thought, without raising his head.

There was some arguing on the other side of the door, and voices that were oddly familiar. Their Yorkshire accents standing out, after all the London witches.

"Mark, y'alright?" Harry hissed so loud, it made his attempt at a whisper pointless.

"Harry, what are you doing here?" Mark asked, pushing himself to his feet. He could see Harry's face on the other side of the small window. His best friend looked red in the face, but otherwise unhurt.

"Hijacking your rescue mission." Harry said, grunting as he tried to force the handle. "It won't shift…"

"It's locked with magic." A bitter voice broke through.

"Michelle?"

"Who else? This was not the plan. I tried to let Harry and Sarah go, but they insisted you were all a bloody package deal."

Mark felt the air around the door shimmer, as the spell was countered. A moment later, the door was yanked open to reveal Mark's friends and a surlier-than-ever Michelle.

"I *knew* there'd be an 'alohomora' spell!" Sarah gloated.

Mark tackled them in a bear hug.

"Escape now, hug later." Michelle snapped. She didn't wait for them, and marched off down the corridor, checking every corner for the rest of her coven.

Mark brought up the rear, not sure what he could actually do with his magic blocked. He followed the others out into the courtyard, they stayed close to the edge, moving in the shadows. They'd have to make a run for it, when they got to the gate, Mark couldn't remember much shelter when they first came in.

Before they got anywhere near the main gate, a shout went up, as the dark witches raised the alarm.

"They've escaped!"

Michelle halted in her tracks, Sarah running into the back of her at the sudden stop.

"C'mon, we might get out through the old water gate." Michelle hissed.

She led back the way they'd come, keeping low. The trio of friends followed her, having no better option.

There was noise and further shouting, followed by a bright burst. One of the dark witches sent up a dazzling source of light, which chased away every shadow.

Mark cowered as their hiding place was stripped of its comforting shadow. It wasn't long before they were spotted. A dozen of Edith's coven members circled them, their magic poised and ready to attack as soon as their leader commanded it.

Mark tried to draw on his own magic again, but it still refused to respond. Mark sighed, and raised his fists, he wouldn't go down without a fight.

The coven members parted, as Edith strode towards the runaways, with Robert in tow. The dark witch looked vaguely amused at their attempt to escape. As she looked towards Michelle, Mark thought he saw Edith's gaze falter. She had clearly not been expecting her newest recruit to betray her. The look was fleeting, but deadly.

"It is close enough to midnight; I don't think we can risk leaving you alive any longer. Shall we begin?" Edith announced to her coven.

The dark witch closed her eyes and chanted foreign words that made Mark's blood run cold. The shadows twisted into a black knife, with a long, curved blade. When Edith raised it, the blade didn't glint or gleam, it sucked in all light.

The coven moved restlessly, eager for what came next.

Robert stepped away from the group, calling a ball of fire into his bare hand, the red glow making him look more demonic than ever.

"You want first shot, Robert?" Edith asked, a flash of confusion crossing her face.

Robert stood staring into the fire he had created. "I have completed the terms of our deal, Edith." He caressed the fire, pushing more demonic energy into it. "Now, I'm bored."

Without warning, he threw the fireball at Mark.

Chapter Nineteen

Mark shouted in surprise, throwing himself aside. The heat was intense as it flew past, singing his sleeve. Mark felt someone tugging at his coat, and looked up to see Harry motioning behind them.

A cool breeze blew through the gaping hole in the wall, the bricks crumbling into ash, to reveal the dark river beyond.

Mark and his friends didn't waste a moment, they ran, stumbling across the debris.

As soon as they crossed the wall, Mark felt his magic return with a joyous surge. It made him feel powerful, he wanted to stop and fight the dark witches on his terms now; but his priority was getting his friends away from danger. He threw up a barrier spell behind them, to slow the dark witches down, as they ran further down the riverside.

Luka reappeared at his side, and the dog raced ahead, leading the way to safety.

Mark was vaguely aware of dark magic pounding against the barrier. With the light of the full moon and the spike of adrenaline, the spell was super-fuelled. Despite this, it would only last so long, before Edith and her coven broke out. As for Robert... there was no guessing which side he was on.

Mark ran alongside the dark river, the fine gravel shifting under his feet. They no longer had a demon to travel the demon road back to Yorkshire; they'd have to get the train, tube, or anything that was available, to get out of Edith's territory.

There was an unearthly scream and Mark's barrier spell was shattered. The dark witches poured out; Mark could feel their demon-fuelled magic stirring all around them. In his paranoia, he thought he saw the shadows moving, racing past and circling them.

At the front of their mis-matched pack, Luka stopped, his intelligent eyes following the movement too.

"Luka, protect the others." Mark ordered, as he tried to focus on creating a new barrier.

The dark coven stopped at it, but Edith didn't hesitate. With a dizzying surge of power, she blasted through Mark's flimsy attempt at a protection spell.

"Did you really think it would be that easy?" Edith snapped, looking distinctly less amused now.

Spells were flying in their direction, dangerously close to his friends, but Mark guessed they were missing on purpose. The dark coven were trying to incite fear, still not seeing them as a threat, because what could a handful of teens possibly do against their demonic magic.

Edith hit him with another debilitating spell, that sent Mark to his knees. It wasn't as paralysing as the last time, as Mark's magic naturally rose up in defence. He managed to look up, focussing on the dark witch.

"East wind blow; east wind howl…" Mark started to chant.

"Really? You're going to use *elemental* magic against me?" Edith sneered.

"Bend to my will; *I summon thee.*"

The wind stirred, rising up at Mark's command. It started to pull at his clothing, a hint of what it was building up to. With a roar, it descended, knocking back the dark witches, who were forced to drop their own spells.

Edith stood, stubbornly leaning into wind. As she concentrated on blocking it, she dropped the spell that had been torturing Mark.

"Do you think…" Edith growled. "You can stop me with a basic elemental spell? Pathetic boy, I can see how it drains you."

"What are you doing?" Michelle hissed at his side, the only other witch in Mark's group, she could probably see the same thing.

Mark could feel the magic exhausting him. The wild winds would soon die. He could sense the edge of control Nanna had warned him to stay away from. Mark glanced

160

over at the dark river. "I'm trusting my instincts." He said, coolly.

Mark felt the edge of the elemental magic flare up in warning, but he pushed more energy into it, taking the spell way beyond safety. The wind stuttered, then died.

With the wind no longer battering her, Edith stood tall again, a disdainful smirk on her lips. The smile faltered, as she looked into the darkness where something else built.

The river shrank back from the shore, the water rustling through the gravel. Everything seemed to pause, then there was a rumble in the distance. It became louder, and Mark could make out the white foam breaking at the top a dark wave that tore down the river.

The water swelled and thundered up the bank. Mark and his friends jumped back as the cold, stinking water closed about their legs. The river rose like a giant water serpent and pounded the shore.

Mark and his friends dashed back towards the street, as the screams went up from the dark witches washed away by the sudden flood.

"ENOUGH!" Edith roared, as she pulled herself back onto land, utterly soaked through. Her magic responded to her anger, heating the water, until steam rose from her wet garments.

Mark's knees shook from his previous exertion, he had nothing left to give. He looked to his friends and Michelle. "Go. I'll distract her."

"No." Harry growled, grabbing Mark's sleeve.

Before Mark could argue, there was a brilliant flash, as lightning hit the deserted road behind them. Mark blinked away the brief, burning pain, his hope stirring once more. The cavalry had arrived. Out stepped Nanna, quickly followed by Denise, Danny, and the rest of their coven. Mark's relief was cut short when he spotted Eadric behind them.

"No…"

"This was my choice." Eadric stated, his green eyes burning intensely. "I was made t' fight, not sit idly by."

Denise drifted past Mark, touching his shoulder. With the brief contact, he felt his energy renewed, and he gave a grateful smile to the kooky witch.

The new arrivals filled the air with magic, forcing the dark coven back. Mark had seen them at work before, but he was still in awe at how powerful his fellow witches were.

Nanna was facing off with Edith, one dark-haired and one grey, both were surrounded by a dizzying power. Mark had once thought that no one could compare to his Nanna, but he feared that Edith was just as strong.

Robert appeared behind the dark coven, practically blazing with demonic energy. He thrust his hands down, and the earth rumbled.

Mark jumped back as the ground spilt beneath his feet, fire bursting up between the gaps. It continued to fracture and grow, causing the witches to lose their focus on the fight.

Mark scrambled to keep his balance, as he slipped closer to the burning inferno. He could sense the demon magic fuelling the flames, which licked threatening close.

Cracks went up the embankment, shooting across the bridge. Great hunks of stone fell, hitting dark and light witches alike. Further cries of pain went up into the night.

Mark felt the shards of stone hit his shoulder, before a shadow passed overhead. He raised his head, no time to avoid the crumbling bridge heading straight for him.

Chapter Twenty

Something hard rammed into Mark's side, and the breath was knocked out of him. The hunk of bridge fell with a resounding crash, the air thick with stone dust. Everyone else disappeared behind the cloud of dust, leaving just Mark and his saviour.

"E-Eadric?" Mark coughed, shaking his shoulder.

Eadric didn't move.

"Eadric?" Mark repeated, panic leaping to his throat.

He didn't need to worry, he told himself. Mark had seen Silvaticus turn boulders into a monster, and beat the crap out of his enemies. A bridge was nothing. Not even a whole bridge, a part-bridge…

The nonsensical thoughts went round and round in Mark's head, as the realisation dawned…

"No!" He cried, as he tried to shift the great lump of rock. If Mark just got it off, Eadric would be alright.

Someone grabbed Mark's arm, pulling him away from the scene of the accident.

"No, you have to save him. He's hurt." Mark yanked back his arm and knelt down next to Eadric. In the shadowy light, he could see the fine stone dust masking Eadric's long brown hair with grey. His eyes were closed, surely he was just knocked out.

Mark reached tentatively towards Eadric, and he was shocked to see his hand shaking badly.

"It's too late, he's gone." Nanna insisted, her voice breaking through the haze. "Come on, we have to get you home."

Mark looked around, his coven and friends stood looking dazed, with various degrees of injuries. There was no sign of the dark witches, or Robert. The fires and floods were dying down, leaving destruction in its wake.

Harry and Sarah looked pale, and were getting checked over by Denise. Mark was glad to see they were still in one piece.

Danny made his way to the fallen bridge. He knelt beside Eadric's body, looking very solemn. Danny hesitantly touched his face, his fingers shaking at the death of his new friend.

With a spell Mark didn't recognise, the witch shifted the rubble, throwing it aside with ease. Danny picked up Eadric. He looked peaceful, as though sleeping, except for the off angle of his limbs.

"Let's go home." Nanna said quietly.

She still held onto Mark's arm, and the rest of their party clustered close together, holding hands in preparation for what was to come. It dawned on Mark that they no longer had a demon, to travel the demon road...

"*Sipwegas*." A man's voice echoed over the group, followed by another lightning bolt.

After the suffocating stillness of the demon road, they returned to the field behind Mark's house. The cool breeze was refreshing after a night in the city.

The coven stood quietly, getting over their disorientation after their unusual method of travel.

"I never thought I'd travel the demon road." Nanna remarked, her voice oddly flat.

"First time for everything." Denise replied, squeezing Nanna's arm.

"I'm getting too old for 'first' anythings." Her banter was without humour, a force of habit.

"W-what now?" Mark asked, hoarsely.

"You need to rest." Nanna stated, focussing on the basics. "And the coven needs to heal."

She nodded to the other witches, who cradled their injuries and made their goodbyes, somewhat solemn after the events of the night.

Mark watched the proceedings numbly, unable to feel anything beyond shock.

"Your friends can kip at mine, tonight... or what's left of tonight." Nanna said to Mark.

"Erm... I'm not a friend." Michelle said bitterly, too tired to even follow it up with her usual sneer.

Nanna stood looking at the angry teenager. "You must be Michelle."

"What if I am?" She snapped defensively.

"Hmph. You can take the spare bedroom, if you don't fancy bunking with the others." Nanna replied.

Michelle stood, dazed at Nanna's offer. As the others made their way to the house, she was the last to follow.

Once inside the warm kitchen, Nanna made them all hot drinks. Mark recognised Nanna's healing tea, but he didn't want soothing right now.

"I've added a sleeping draught, to bring on sleep, without dreams." Nanna said, quietly. "Go make yourselves comfortable in the living room, I'll bring blankets."

Mark watched as Harry and Sarah went into the other room as instructed. Michelle took a little longer to head upstairs, nursing her mug with a confused look on her face. When Nanna had finished with her hostess duties, she returned to the kitchen table.

"Your tea is getting cold." She remarked, "Want me to warm it up."

Mark stared into the cooling liquid. "He's really dead?"

"Yes."

"It's all my fault. I tried to keep him away." Mark said, his heart breaking.

"It's no one's fault." Nanna argued. "Eadric chose to go to London. He chose to rescue you. I haven't known the young man for long, but I think he would have been proud to die protecting those he loved."

Mark gripped his mug so tightly, his knuckles turned white. "That doesn't make it any better."

"No, but if you felt *anythin'* for Eadric, you have to respect his decisions." Nanna stressed. "You're young, this is the first time you've lost anyone. It's supposed to hurt."

Mark ran a hand through his hair, tempted to tear it out. A physical pain might be easier to deal with.

"Mark, death is a natural, inevitable, part of life. We all have to die; it's what we do with our lives that matters." Nanna said reaching out and gently squeezing his arm.

The thought coherently stringing a sentence together made Mark's head spin, but there was something he had to know. "E-Eadric once told me he didn't fear death; he only feared being trapped in the eternal torture Robert had subjected him to." Mark raised his gaze to meet Nanna's. His eyes felt so dry they itched. "He's definitely...? I mean, how do we know for sure...?"

"Don't worry, lad. He's at rest." Nanna said, firmly.

Mark closed his eyes, a wave of exhaustion hitting him. "That dark witch – Edith – she hates you. She hates me, too. She doesn't even know me, but she's already decided that she hates me so fiercely..."

Nanna stood up, walking round the table, to wrap Mark in a protective hug. "She's driven by hatred. She's so consumed by dark magic, there's no humanity left in her."

"She said... that I was your heir?" Mark asked. "Heir to what?"

"To my whole kingdom!" Nanna gestured to the well-worn kitchen in the old farmhouse. Her joke fell flat. "One day, you'll inherit my powers. One day, you'll take on the mantle of the Grand High Witch."

"What?" Mark asked, pulling back from her hug. "There's other stronger, more experienced witches."

"You're my grandson; the obvious choice." Nanna sighed. "It's about the strength of your soul, not your magic. With any luck, we'll have years to train you up."

Mark twisted in her arms, to look up at his Nanna. She looked tired. His Nanna who burnt with eternal youth and vitality looked *old*, for the first time. The fight tonight must have drained her more than Mark thought.

"Wh-?"

"It's late. Drink your tea and get some sleep." Nanna insisted, wrapping her hand around Mark's mug, causing the tea to heat and steam again.

Chapter Twenty-One

Mark slept the rest of the weekend, and when Ostara dawned on Monday, he was excused from school on account of his religion.

This year would bring no frivolous celebrations. The coven was in no state to have their usual family-friendly festivities. Instead, they'd gathered for a funeral.

The sun was shining brightly on a beautiful warm day, in complete contrast to the sombre mood.

The funeral was held at the ruins of Eadric's house, the witches having marched across the moors, to pay their respects.

Mark made his way with Harry and Sarah in tow. They'd stayed at his house for the rest of the weekend, and now they provided silent support, when he needed them most.

When they reached Eadric's house, the only sign of his abode were the worn stones poking out from the grey-green grass. Mark noticed the stones were silent, now Silvaticus had been released, they no longer whispered to him.

Eadric lay on a roughly-hewn altar that hadn't been there before. Three witches stood in a circle around him, Nanna, Denise and Danny were all ready to start the ceremony. The rest of the coven made a loose circle around him.

As Mark approached, Nanna nodded to him. Mark squeezed Harry's arm in silent thanks, leaving him and Sarah at the edge of the gathering, and made his way instinctively to the South point.

When his feet found the right spot, Mark felt an overwhelming sense of power and balance. Nanna stood solemnly across from him, and even Denise's usually care-free aura was sombre. When he turned his attention to Danny on his right, Mark noticed something was different, but he couldn't put his finger on it.

Behind him, the coven started to chant. Mark felt their power unite, to mourn their lost friend, and to heal those that remained. Mark felt something unlock inside him, and the pain he had been suppressing rushed to the fore. Tears ran down his face, the first time he had cried since Eadric's death. His friend was gone, he had to accept that.

Mark didn't care that he was crying in public, surrounded by the coven that continued to support him. His grief was a part of him that he had to embrace. There was no shame in his tears, and once they washed away the weakness, he felt stronger and more stable.

The chanting culminated in a crescendo of magic, rushing out over the countryside, fuelled by Ostara.

Mark didn't know how long he stood there, as part of the circle, part of his coven; just one piece of a larger creature. It was oddly peaceful, standing with the other witches.

Eventually, Nanna stepped back from the circle, effectively ending the ritual. Mark followed her lead, moving away from the altar.

Only Danny remained, and with another spell Mark didn't recognise, the altar hovered in the air, as the soil beneath it obediently shifted aside. The earth obeyed Danny, until there was a deep hole. The stone altar started to lower, steady and perfectly-controlled.

Mark fixed his gaze on the edge of the altar, he couldn't bring himself to look at Eadric, in case his emotions overwhelmed him again. Instead, he focussed on the rough contours of the stone. It seemed only right that Eadric Stoneman should be buried in such a fashion.

Mark hated to admit that he was impressed by Danny's skills. He knew that Danny was a very powerful witch, but after joining him in a magical circle, Mark had naturally assumed that Danny's elemental preference was water. He'd never guessed that Danny was such an expert controlling earth and rock...

Mark's next thoughts caused goosebumps. He willed himself to stay in the present, and looked one last time at Eadric, tears threatening to spill again.

A moment later, Danny started to slowly move the earth back into its original position, burying their friend.

He seemed to read Mark's mind, and looked up to meet his gaze, Danny's eyes as black as night.

"Silvaticus?"

Mark trembled, not sure what this meant. His Nanna appeared at his side, squeezing his hand gently.

"Are you alright, boy?" She asked, in that special quiet, comforting voice, that seemed reserved for funerals and bad news.

"*Silvaticus is possessing Danny?*" Mark hissed, not sure who knew, or what trouble it might mean.

Nanna blinked, looking over at Danny. She remained completely unruffled by the news.

"Oh that. I know, it was Danny's idea." Nanna looked thoughtfully at Mark. "I guess you missed that part, as you'd already rushed into the middle of Edith's trap."

Mark felt a sting of guilt. No matter how many times he told himself that he had no other choice, it was still painful that his rash actions had led others to be hurt, or worse. "What do you mean? What happened?"

"After you sent Eadric away in your foolish attempt to save him, he went back to Denise's and raised the alarm. She managed to alert the rest of the coven. When I got to her house, Eadric had already decided that he was going after you. The only thing that stopped him using the demon road and going immediately, was his fear of being trapped by Robert, before he had a chance to rescue you. He said that, if he could take some witches with him to London, at least someone would be left to save you." Nanna took a deep breath. "Danny was being his logical self. He theorised that, if Silvaticus was no longer possessing Eadric, then they couldn't be trapped in an eternity of pain together. So, if the worst should happen, Eadric would be free…"

"Silvaticus can just change host like that?" Mark frowned.

Nanna shrugged. "It's not something I've witnessed before, but Silvaticus said it would be straight-forward, especially with a willing host."

A shadow crossed Mark's path, and he looked up to see Danny – no, Silvaticus.

"Silvaticus?"

The demon nodded once, slowly.

"Is Danny… OK?" Mark asked hesitantly.

Silvaticus frowned, not answering immediately. "He will be. Having a mutually-beneficial connection like ours, it's been a shock to his system. Poor Danny also has to negotiate my grief for Eadric."

Mark watched Silvaticus carefully. The demon never seemed to express any emotion. Even now, at the funeral of his previous host, he looked too calm and controlled.

"Do you feel? I mean, do demons feel?" Mark blurted out, before he could stop himself.

174

"Yes." Silvaticus replied quietly. "We feel much more intensely than humans. Some demons, like Robert, thrill in lashing out at the world, in response to these emotions. Others, like me, have become very good at hiding them over the years."

Silvaticus reached out and touched the side of Mark's head. Before Mark could react, he suddenly felt like he was standing at a precipice, with a deep pit of despair waiting before him. He didn't know how he was sharing them, but Mark was sure these were the feelings that ravaged Silvaticus.

Silvaticus removed his hand, and Mark snapped into the present. He gasped, and wiped away the fresh tears that had flooded out.

"I'm sorry, I'm so sorry." He mumbled.

Silvaticus nodded slowly once more, continuing to look the most calm and stable person around.

"I'm... glad you're still here." Mark confessed.

"Thank you, Mark." Silvaticus paused. "I still have unfinished business. I am too exhausted from this weekend, but I need to kill Robert – for Eadric's sake."

Chapter Twenty-Two

Mark noticed that there was no sign of Damian at the funeral, or after, when they all piled into Denise's house for drinks and a buffet.

It seemed odd, seeing so many people in head-to-toe black, making Denise's home look even more colourful by contrast.

Mark found himself standing by the kitchen table, his hand resting on the warm wood surface. He'd been sitting there when Eadric had stunned him by walking out shirtless. He'd sat there with Eadric several times, his friend's warmth a real and steady thing.

Now he was gone, and never coming back. It didn't make sense to Mark.

"You OK, kiddo?" Denise asked, as she brought out more sandwiches. Her bright-turquoise hair was tucked away behind a black lace headscarf.

"Yeah." Mark replied shortly.

"No, you're not." Denise looked at him knowingly. "But you will be."

Mark shrugged, unable to come up with any response that didn't include nonsense, swearing, or both. All he wanted was to get out of here, and see Damian, before he had to return to the enforced imprisonment of school tomorrow.

When Denise moved on to check on her guests' drinks, Mark slunk away. No one would miss him. Harry and Sarah had disappeared into the garden half an hour ago, and could have gone home, for all Mark knew.

Letting himself out the front door, Mark marched down the driveway and started walking in the direction of Damian's house. The day was very pleasant for this time of year, with a warm breeze and a bright sun overhead. A mile down the road, Mark was beginning to regret his hasty decision. It would have been quicker if he'd gone home and got his bike. Now he'd take forever to get to his boyfriend's and have the bonus of turning up in a sweaty mess.

There was the sharp honk of a car horn, that made Mark jump. He turned to see a vaguely-familiar red Audi, pulling up beside him.

"Need a lift?" Miriam called out. "I'm guessing you're heading to our place."

Mark got in the car gratefully, a slight smile that Miriam was now almost-officially part of Damian's family. "Yes, thanks."

The car glided away smoothly, and the two of them settled into an uncomfortable silence. It seemed to Mark that every time he spoke to Miriam, he was getting accused of doing the wrong thing. He wondered how long it would take-

"I can't believe you acted so foolishly again." Miriam remarked. "Especially after I warned you, and Nanna warned you."

"I didn't have much of a choice. Give me a break." Mark argued. "You're not my guardian, or *my* aunt-to-be. You're not even Damian's yet."

"I'm not..." Miriam snapped, then hesitated. "Sorry, that came out wrong, I'm not used to talking to teenagers."

Mark eyed her warily, not sure how else he could interpret her comments.

Miriam gave a heavy sigh. "I'm not trying to be a figure of authority. I'm trying to be a *friend* and a coven-mate."

"Oh." Mark felt guilty for his earlier defence.

"Yes, 'oh'. You don't always know best, Mark."

Mark pulled at a loose thread on his shirt cuff. "At least I'm not completely clueless – did you see the news article about the 'freak storm' in London on Saturday night?" Mark rolled his eyes.

Miriam laughed, the tension in the car dropping away. "Yeah, you've gotta love the imagination of non-witches. Bleedin' muggles!"

Mark chanced a glance at Miriam, it was nice to see her be less-than-professional for a few minutes. "How's Miss Cole – I mean, Maggie – after this weekend?"

"She's fine. She accepted I was involved in a coven emergency, even though she didn't grasp the seriousness of it. She assumed that Damian stayed over with you, she didn't realise he was in London, too. He turned up on Sunday, pretending nothing happened." Miriam glanced over at Mark. "The sooner Damian tells her the truth, the better. I'm getting fed up with lying to her."

"I'm working on it." Mark replied, as they pulled up at Maggie's cottage.

Maggie sent Mark straight on through to Damian's room. He'd barely finished knocking when his boyfriend yanked the door open, and pulled him in.

"Hey."

"Hey..." Damian leant forward, to kiss him, but thought better and pulled back again, awkwardly.

"Miriam said you got back yesterday OK." Mark shrugged. "You didn't text."

"Um, yeah. When my parents died, I remember how much I just needed space from everyone. I didn't want to intrude, until you were ready for me to... be there..." Damian mumbled. "Whatever happened this weekend, Robert brought me back to the village. I'm surprised he had the energy, he feels even more exhausted than last time."

"Are you... OK?" Mark asked, guilty that he'd dragged his boyfriend into such a dangerous situation.

"Is it weird that I am?" Damian frowned. "I dunno, maybe it's 'cos Robert's so weak; but I feel great!"

"Huh." Mark didn't know enough about demons to venture a guess, and honestly couldn't begrudge Damian of all people, feeling good for once. "I... thought I'd see you at the funeral, today."

"I didn't think it would be a good idea to attend." Damian looked embarrassed. "I look too much like Robert."

"Oh." Mark was surprised. He wasn't sure what excuse he was expecting from his boyfriend, but it hadn't been that.

"I don't know what actually happened on Saturday, or... if Robert responsible for Eadric's death?" Damian asked, shakily.

"No!" Mark grabbed him and drew him into a hug, feeling Damian tremble in his arms. "A lot happened that night. It was no one's fault."

Mark couldn't persuade himself, though. He carried his guilt with him. If he hadn't gone to London; if he'd made more effort to stop Eadric, his friend might still be alive.

Damian curled into him, finding comfort in his presence. When he spoke, his voice was muffled. "I'm so relieved to hear that... I was terrified the witches would want revenge on me... him... us..."

180

Damian raised his head to look deep into Mark's eyes. "I'm not sure what the correct pronouns are, I'm scared that we're blurring."

Mark traced the contours of Damian's face, the sharp cheekbones, and soft lips. "I see *you*, Damian. You will *never* be Robert in my eyes, or that of the witches."

Mark pressed his lips lightly against Damian's, a brief promise.

"I love you."

Other books by K.S. Marsden:

Witch-Hunter ~ Now available in audiobook
The Shadow Rises (Witch-Hunter #1)
The Shadow Reigns (Witch-Hunter #2)
The Shadow Falls (Witch-Hunter #3)

Witch-Hunter trilogy box-set

Witch-Hunter Prequels
James: Witch-Hunter (#0.5)
Sophie: Witch-Hunter (#0.5)
Kristen: Witch-Hunter (#2.5) ~ coming 2021

Enchena
The Lost Soul: Book 1 of Enchena
The Oracle: Book 2 of Enchena

Northern Witch
Winter Trials (Northern Witch #1)
Awaken (Northern Witch #2)
The Breaking (Northern Witch #3)
Summer Sin (Northern Witch #4)

Read on for a sneak peek at the next part of the
Northern Witch series -
Summer Sin…

Chapter One

Mark picked absent-mindedly at the black material of his funeral clothes. His best trousers were stiff and uncomfortable, but some discomfort seemed in keeping with the day.

Only a few hours ago, they had been attending Eadric's funeral, with a dozen witches and friends showing their respect for the pagan ritual.

At the time, Mark had been honoured to be a part of it, and had found solace amongst his coven. But as soon as it was over, he could feel the grief of losing Eadric nipping at his heels. Mark already missed his bright green eyes, and his gentle innocence... gone forever because Mark was foolish enough to drag him into the middle of a witch war.

Mark had tried to keep busy and distract himself, first with his coven; and then visiting Damian in the afternoon, allowing his boyfriend to be his sole focus.

Now though, as Miriam drove him home in silence, stray thoughts plucked at Mark's mind. Eadric's easy smile, and the surprising roughness of his skin when his hand brushed against Mark's.

It was starting to get dark by the time Miriam dropped Mark off, in front of the big farmhouse that was home.

"If you ever need anyone to speak to..." Miriam trailed off. Despite protesting that she was trying to be his friend, she probably knew that teenage-Mark had a slew of friends his own age... "Fine, go, do your thing."

Mark tried to smile his thanks, he knew Miriam was only trying to be nice, but it came off as a bit of an awkward grimace. "I do appreciate it." He said, letting himself out of the car.

The spring evening was mild and calm, and Mark was in no rush to go inside, back to real life. He watched and waved as Miriam's red Audi disappeared down the drive.

When he moved back to the house, movement caught Mark's eye, as a curtain opened in an upstairs window. A pale face hovered, glowering down at him.

"What the-?"

Mark barged through Nanna's empty kitchen, racing up the stairs, two at a time. His initial bravery faded, and he tentatively pushed open the door to the spare room, wary of the monster within.

"Michelle?"

"No, it's sodding Voldemort. Who did you expect?" Came the waspy reply.

Michelle looked her usual angry self, scowling at Mark for daring to exist, never mind his audacity at being in her vicinity.

"Uh, don't take this the wrong way, but why are you here?" Mark asked.

"Why do you think? Your psycho Nanna has kept me trapped in this house since we got back from London!"

"What? Why?"

186

"She's worried I might go off the rails or cast dark magic." Michelle growled. Holding out her hands, her frown deepened. "I can't... I can't draw on my magic in this prison. She's even blocked reception for my phone – I haven't been able to call for help!"

Mark paused; he knew how that felt. Only a few days ago, he'd had the freakish experience of having his magic out of reach.

"You need to get me out of here." Michelle demanded.

"What... no."

Michelle's eyes widened in disbelief. "Seriously? I risked everything to rescue you from London; you owe me."

"Er... this is nothing alike. You rescued me from a bunch of crazy witches who beat me up and were about to kill me." Mark replied, the bruises were still achingly fresh. "You're stuck with Nanna – who at worst, will overfeed you tea and biscuits."

"I'm still trapped against my will." Michelle snapped, snatching up one of the porcelain figures from the windowsill and throwing it at Mark.

It smashed into the door frame, and Mark backed away from her angry outburst, not wanting to test her throwing skills any further. "OK, OK. I'll see what I can do." He said, holding his hands up defensively.

Mark kept one eye on Michelle, and walked sideways down the stairs. He wouldn't put it past her to push him down the narrow staircase.

"Nanna...?" Under Michelle's scrutiny, his voice wavered. Mark coughed and called again. "Nanna!"

The living room door opened, and Nanna stepped through, still wearing her black funeral clothes.

"What's up, kiddo?" She asked innocently.

"What's up?" Mark echoed. "How about the bloody Wicked Witch of the West trapped in your house?"

Nanna glanced up the stairs, spotting Michelle hovering on the landing. "She's dangerous."

Michelle looked a little smug at the description.

"To us, and herself." Nanna amended. "We can't let a witch juiced up on dark magic loose."

"So, Michelle is going to stay here forever?" Mark asked.

"Not forever." Nanna shrugged. "She's new to dark magic, I'm hoping her addiction won't take long to break."

"You're forgetting, you old bat, I don't want your help." Michelle snapped.

"You say the nicest things." Nanna replied. "Mark, can you please bring Michelle's schoolwork home with you tomorrow. Then you can both train in white magic in the evening."

"What!" Both exclaimed.

Mark was used to having Nanna to himself, and he wasn't sure how he felt sharing her with this angry girl who was pissed off at the world.

"This is pointless, just let me go you crazy witch." Michelle barrelled down the stairs, her murderous glare fixed on Nanna.

"Nanna, watch... out..." Mark's warning faded.

Nanna threw up a hand with a careless gesture and Michelle stopped, stuck behind an invisible barrier. The girl's mouth was opened in scream and slammed her fists against the magical blockade, all noise blocked.

"Thanks for the warning, Mark." Nanna said drily. "I don't know what I would have done if you weren't here."

Mark grunted in response to her sarcasm. "Is this the part where you brag what a powerful witch you are?"

"Well, you do seem to need reminding frequently." Nanna remarked, then nodded in Michelle's direction, where the young girl was still flailing wildly. "She's been having these outbursts all weekend; they fade after a few minutes. We'll be back to sullen teenage silence in no time."

"Holding someone against their will is illegal." Mark pointed out.

"They weren't thinking of magical rehab when they made those rules. Besides, I spoke to Michelle's *legal guardians*." Nanna rolled her eyes. "Her parents didn't even notice she was missing."

On the other side of the invisible barrier, Michelle's tantrum began to fade, just as Nanna predicted. The girl looked exhausted; her rage dissipated into nothing.

"It's late, you should get home before your parents ground you again."

Chapter Two

The next day at school, Mark felt like he was the centre of attention, yet again. It seemed to be the new norm: in the winter term, everyone thought he had used dark magic to attack his classmates; and last term they all thought he'd been cheating on his boyfriend – who was coincidentally their new star striker.

Mark winced as he caught sight of his reflection in one of the windows. He was a bruised and battered mess. The lump on his head was going down, but there was no way to hide the graze across his jaw, and the wicked purple bruise on his face.

Mark wondered what story his classmates would make up this time; it was sure to be good. At least this time, Mark had his supporters back in place.

His best friends, Harry and Sarah, walked ahead. They were being extra-loud, to prove how extra-normal this was. And his boyfriend Damian stood at Mark's side, his fingers nervously brushing his hand.

They had held hands on dates before, and Mark wondered if Damian would dare to do the same at school, especially now they were on a new level. Mark blushed again, as he relived last night, when he'd admitted he was in love with Damian.

Damian hadn't said it back yet, but everything suddenly seemed more serious.

Mark headed to his morning tutor group, and a piece of paper was thrust into his hand.

"Exam timetable?" He read, his heart dropping.

"Yes, we went over it at length, yesterday." His form tutor replied. "I don't know if you remember, but you have your final GSCE exams next month."

Mark rolled his eyes. He couldn't forget if he tried. All his teachers had drilled them over their exams, as though it was news. Mark had lost the will for any original response. "Yes sir." He managed.

"If you have any questions, you know where to find me."

"Yes sir." Mark repeated.

Knowing that he didn't have the teen's attention, his tutor waved a hand to dismiss him.

Mark wasn't allowed to forget about his exams for a second as, when his tutor session drew to a close, every single class and teacher hammered it home. They droned on about the final countdown, and structuring revision, and taking responsibility for yourself.

Mark's head was thumping. He was relieved to make it to dinnertime, and a whole hour's break. He'd no sooner set his tray down at his usual table, than he overheard his fellow students debating the best approach to revision. Mark groaned and dropped his head on the table.

"You alright?"

Mark looked up to see his boyfriend sliding into the chair next to him. "Have you heard: the exams are coming."

Damian bit back a smile. "It might've been mentioned."

"If anyone mentions exams in the next hour, I will stab them with my fork." Sarah warned, waving her blunt weapon.

"Noted." Mark grinned at the threat posed by the petite blonde girl.

"In more important news, *before* we got kidnapped by dark witches and threatened with death and torture..." Sarah announced with a dismissive wave of her hand. "Harry totally rocked on stage, and his fan-base is growing!"

"That's awesome." Mark replied, his voice not quite sounding right. He was thrilled that Harry's fledgling singing career was taking off, but he couldn't forget that the dark witches and their death threats his friends had suffered were all his fault.

Edith and her coven had only kidnapped Harry and Sarah to lure Mark out of hiding. Mark had a long way to go before he made it up to his friends. It was already too late to make it up to Eadric...

Mark felt pressure on his arm, and he saw Damian leaning against him, a look of concern crossing his face.

"I'm fine." Mark insisted.

Harry didn't seem to notice the exchange; he was too busy listing the venues that his 'manager' was negotiating with. "The Warehouse in Leeds have already asked me to come back, and there's loads'a places in Sheffield I want to perform."

Mark forced a weak smile; he could well believe that Harry wanted to do a gig in the hometown of his favourite band. Hell, Harry probably already saw himself warming up for the Artic Monkeys.

"Anywhere but London..." Harry pulled a face. "We've learnt our lesson – no more venues owned by demons, or in league with evil witches. My manager is going to do thorough background checks from now on."

"Sounds like a lotta work."

Sarah smiled adoringly at her boyfriend. "He's worth it."

"Wow, I've never seen the mushy thing up close." Damian hissed in Mark's ear. "You're right, they're very intense."

Mark snorted a laugh, receiving weird looks from his friends. "Y'know, you still owe Dean a gig."

"What?"

"He was at the gig in Leeds – he promised not to tell the other students, if you'd perform at his next party." Mark saw their confusion change to concern. "Sorry, I thought I'd told you."

"Nah, you were too busy making eyes at Eadric." Harry broke off when he received a less-than-subtle punch from Sarah. "Oh, is that the time? We have to, um..."

Harry stood up, his empty plate rattling on the table. Sarah escorted him briskly out of the food hall, before he could embarrass them any further.

"Well, that was uncomfortable." Mark remarked, his humour not hitting the right note.

"Look, I don't judge you for anything that happened after I broke up with you." Damian said. He sounded sincere, but he didn't raise his eyes from the table.

"*Nothing* happened..." Mark stressed. Maybe if he said it often enough, he'd believe it too.

*****

Mark headed home, with his rucksack digging into his shoulder, as he tried to fit two bulky folders in it. Both folders contained a breakdown of the exams. Mark wondered how long it would be before Michelle threw her copy out of the window. He didn't know why Nanna insisted that he brought Michelle's work home, there wasn't a chance in hell that she'd do anything more productive than turn it into confetti.

Mark made his way into Nanna's kitchen, the kettle already boiling on the Aga, and a plate of biscuits on the table.

Michelle came stomping down the stairs as Mark poured the tea. Her brow raised disdainfully. "This is too cute." She muttered, pinching a biscuit.

"You don't have to be here."

Michelle snorted. "Have you forgotten that I'm trapped in this house? What am I supposed to do, stay in my bedroom until your Nanna magically decides to release me?"

It wasn't *her* bedroom, Mark wanted to argue, a new and surprising territorial feeling over his family's house.

"It's fine." Mark replied curtly. "I brought your homework."

Michelle ignored the folder that was dumped on the table, her dark-brown eyes were fixed on Mark with an unsettling gaze.

"That passive-aggressive thing don't work." She stated. "You keep sayin' you're fine, but you never mean it – I can see your anger, and so can everyone else."

"I'm not angry-"

"Fine; frustrated, upset, in pain..." Michelle interjected. "Your fella died. Why even pretend you're OK?"

The dark energy that had been bubbling inside Mark all day surged up again. His coven had paid tribute to Eadric at yesterday's pagan funeral, which had provided a temporary boon.

Now that he acknowledged its existence, the darkness threatened to rush back. The pain, the grief, and the guilt that Eadric had given his life to save Mark.

"My coven helped start the healing." He argued.

Michelle snorted inelegantly. "Save all that touchy-feely crap. What you really need is to scream."

"What?" Mark blurted out.

"Don't look at me gone out." Michelle protested. "It ain't illegal. Dare you to scream."

A strangled noise came out of Mark's throat, before he coughed and blushed. "I don't think-"

Michelle interrupted him with an ear-splitting scream.

Once Mark got over his shock, he felt the pressure rise to join in. He started to scream, pathetic at first, his voice wobbling, before he put some oomph behind it.

Michelle caught his eye and they both broke into laughter.

The dark part that had been stirring now settled back down, sated for now.

"You were right, it worked." Mark confessed.

Michelle nodded; her smile being replaced by her usual sneer. "Still not your friend." She pointed out.

"What the blazes?"

Mark turned to see Nanna standing in the doorway, looking at them in disbelief.

"I thought someone was bein' murdered."

Mark gulped. "Um, no, Michelle was sharing some stress-relief theories."

Nanna shook her head. "Why can't you just scrap, like normal kids?"

Mark hid his smile behind his cup of tea.

"Right, we're gonna do some basic crystal work today. The moon is still full enough to be useful." Nanna announced. "I've only got one book, so you'll have to share for your homework."

"Share?" Michelle spat. "I'm not doing some namby-pamby white magic."

Nanna crossed her arms. "You are if you ever want to do magic again. We don't allow dark magic around here."

"You don't control me."

197

"Of course I don't, dearie." Nanna replied drily. "I'll just keep you trapped in here, blocked from dark magic, until you change your mind. If it takes months, years... I'm in no rush."

Michelle's usually-pasty complexion whitened further at the threat.

Nanna grabbed a wide wooden box and placed it on the kitchen table. When she opened it, she revealed stones and gems of various colours and shapes.

"Crystals can help bring balance, and provide energy to boost the strength of your spells." Nanna reeled off, gesturing to the box. "Select a crystal, and we'll practise pouring energy into them, for later use."

"This is why dark magic is better. It's strong on its own." Michelle scowled at the box. "These aren't all *crystals* anyway."

"It's a generic term girly." Nanna replied. "And the sooner you pull that stick out of your arse and give it a go, the sooner your lesson will be over."

Mark bit his tongue, there was something satisfying about Nanna taking on the school bully.

He turned to the task, remembering what Nanna had previously told him about the importance of picking your own stone. He felt a pull towards an unpolished garnet with a dark, purplish hue.

Mark watched as Michelle's hand snapped out and picked up a lump of jet.

"Jet is protective by nature, it's a good stone to have." Nanna commented. "Now, call the quarters to create a neutral workspace. Michelle, if you struggle to envision them, you can use elements to back you up."

When Nanna's back was turned, Michelle raised her hand in a rude gesture.

"Y'know the glass cabinet is reflective." Nanna remarked. "Mark, you can help Michelle find her zen."

Both Mark and Michelle groaned loudly.

Nanna made herself comfortable, in the corner of the kitchen, opening her latest copy of Cosmo.

Calling the quarters was becoming easy for Mark, and as he slipped into the zone, a familiar calm greeted him. His attention was forced back to reality, as he saw Michelle glowering at him.

"Y'know, the growly witch routine is getting old." He remarked. "Do you want help?"

"No." Michelle snapped.

"Uh huh, sure." Mark got up from his seat and rummaged around the kitchen, pulling out utensils to represent the elements. A bowl of water for West; a pot of earth and basil to the North; an empty bowl of air to the East. Finally, with a little focus, Mark set a candle alight for the South point.

Michelle watched him with extreme wariness and derision at his reliance on natural magic; but when all the four points were honoured, her eyes fluttered shut. Michelle's breath stilled, and a look of pure peace crossed her face. Without her trademark anger and rage, she looked like a stranger.

Mark could sense the little jet stone drawing out her darkness like a poison.

Michelle jolted away, looking accusingly at Mark. Panic fuelled her brown eyes.

Michelle pushed her chair back, the legs screeching across the tile floor. She fled upstairs without a word, leaving Mark sitting alone in stunned silence.

Nanna put down her magazine, gazing curiously at the aftermath.

"What...?"

"Jet protects against darkness; it also helps balance and heal the soul." Nanna gave a bitter smile. "Poor Michelle, being at peace is a completely foreign concept to her. No wonder she freaked out."

Mark stared at the empty chair next to him. He didn't understand Michelle, she actively chose the darkest path. The school bully, the dark witch, the demon's mistress. She only had herself to blame.

"She could do with a friend right now." Nanna prompted.

Knowing how futile it was to argue, Mark snatched up the abandoned black stone and stomped upstairs. He knocked on the spare bedroom door.

"Sod off."

Mark braced himself for further thrown knick-knacks, as he opened the door. This time, Michelle was sat quietly on the single bed, with a very familiar ginger cat in her lap.

"Traitor!" Mark gasped.

"What?" Michelle was so surprised, a hurt expression slipped past her mask.

"No, not you." Mark said, gesturing to the cat. "Tigger."

"Is that his name?" Michelle scratched him under the chin. "He's been keeping me company for the last couple of days. At least he doesn't judge me, do you, pretty boy?"

Mark watched the bizarre scene of the big-bad-bully cooing to the fluffy cat. Tigger purred, enjoying the attention thoroughly.

"We're only trying to help." Mark said gently.

"Well, be less helpful."

Mark leant against the doorframe. "How did you get tangled up in demons and dark magic?"

"Robert found me. He opened my eyes to the real world. After years of feeling like I was living a false life, he offered me the truth, and to connect with my real family." Michelle shrugged. "For a price."

"Yeah, he likes his bargains." Mark muttered. "What did you have to do, use dark magic for him?"

"Hell no, that was my prize. You can be as judgy as you like, but dark magic was power, in a world where I'd always been powerless. I didn't care where it came from." Michelle rolled her eyes. "No, Robert wanted my help. It started with little stuff, bringing him up-to-date after his stint in demon prison. Teaching him to use a phone, y'know."

"And then?"

Michelle hugged Tigger closer to her chest, staring resolutely at the wall.

"Was it worth it?"

Michelle gave a weird tilt of her head. "He followed through on his side of the bargain. Trained me up in dark magic, and delivered me to my mother."

"But-?" Mark frowned, not following the logic. As far as he recalled, her parents lived in Tealford. Mark had seen her mother working at the local bank, and knew she had nothing to do with witchcraft.

"I'm adopted." Michelle mumbled.

"I had no idea!"

"Well, it's not bleedin' public knowledge." Michelle snapped with a reassuring bite. "I've always known. Dunno why my parents took me in, they don't give two shits about me. I tried to find info on my birth parents, but no luck. Then Robert turned up with stories about my birth-mother."

"Oh... um, cool?" Mark said weakly, not knowing what the standard response was supposed to be. "So... was your mum part of Edith's coven?"

Michelle gave him a dead stare, waiting for him to catch up.

The penny finally dropped.

"Edith?"

Michelle gave a slow nod, focussing on the warm cat again.

"Woah." No wonder Mark had thought that Edith looked familiar. In fact, with her dark brown hair and slightly-cruel aura, he wondered how he'd missed it. "Who else knows?"

"No one. I don't really want to advertise that I'm the spawn of the witch that nearly killed everyone." Michelle scowled at him. "If you tell anyone, I'll kill you."

"Noted." Mark rolled the lump of jet in his palm. "Here, you forgot this."

He placed it on her dresser, the black stone looking small and innocent.

"I know that using natural magic isn't as flashy as your demon-fuelled stuff, but I think you should give it a go." Mark shrugged. "Besides, it'd be nice not to be the only witch-in-training here."

Summer Sin is available in ebook & paperback.

Printed in Great Britain
by Amazon

69671854R00119